Praise for

HOLLY JACOBS

"The perfect combination of heartwarming
romance and hilarious comedy!"
—*USA TODAY* bestselling author Lori Foster

"...more laughs than should be legal."
—Kelley Hartsell, *Love Romances*

"Holly Jacobs'...*Found and Lost* is a delight.
A darkly comic whodunit, it's her best book yet."
—Catherine Witmer, *Romantic Times BOOKclub*

SPOTLIGHT

HOLLY JACOBS

Confessions of a Party Crasher

HARLEQUIN®

TORONTO • NEW YORK • LONDON
AMSTERDAM • PARIS • SYDNEY • HAMBURG
STOCKHOLM • ATHENS • TOKYO • MILAN • MADRID
PRAGUE • WARSAW • BUDAPEST • AUCKLAND

ISBN 0-373-83707-0

CONFESSIONS OF A PARTY CRASHER

Susan thanks for the brainstorming.
Kathryn and Alethea, thanks for the encouragement
and for helping make this book happen. And for Jessica,
Katie and Abbey...daughters who know just how my heroine
in *Confessions of a Party Crasher* feels. Thanks for putting
up with me and even hanging with me on purpose!
A mother couldn't ask for smarter, sweeter, funnier
daughters (not that I'm biased or anything)!
I love you all!

PROLOGUE

MORGAN MILLER WOULD FOREVER think of this particular dance as the funeral wake tango, an inventive attempt at avoidance.

Every time *they* moved in her direction, she countered. Step for step—watching, analyzing, moving from one group to another.

If she wanted to play the optimist, there was an upside. Avoiding *them* kept her mind off her loss.

But to be honest, Morgan wasn't feeling the least bit optimistic. As a matter of fact, she was downright pessimistic at the moment.

She knew where she'd like to lay the blame, but in all fairness, there was more to it than just *them*. However, not totally blaming them didn't mean she wanted to talk to them, thereby allowing them to salve their troubled collective consciences.

They—a nauseating twosome, joined at the hip—moved as a single unit intent on cornering her.

If she'd been in league with them, she'd have told them they might have better luck splitting up and attacking from opposite directions. But she wasn't.

Together they started in her direction again.

Morgan was scanning for a new group to join, one that was preferably as far from *them* as she could get, when her mother cleared her throat from the front of the church hall.

Morgan was thankful her mom, for at least the moment, had stopped her own prowling of the wake. Unlike Morgan's would-be stalkers, Annabelle was going after every single man present, regardless of age.

She cleared her throat again, then started. "Auggie didn't want this to be a time of mourning. He wanted this to be a celebration of his life. So if everyone could grab a glass, let's raise it to August Banyon, a wonderful friend, employer, neighbor…a hell of a guy."

Morgan forgot about her ex-fiancé and her ex-best friend and raised her glass, toasting the man who'd been a friend, a mentor and a surrogate, benevolent uncle.

Slowly, as if it had been scripted, the mourners began to share stories about Auggie. Some to the entire room, some in small groups.

Morgan was still doing her peculiar dance, so she caught snippets from every section of the room as she moved around.

"…and that dog. I never met such a humper. Every time I walked in the door, he eyed my legs…."

"…I thought his cats were creepy. He said they were shy, but they just lurked around the house, spying on us…"

"…and he still watched every rerun of *Gilligan's Island*…."

"…such a laugh."

"…zest for life."

"…never forgot his Ethel. I want that kind of love someday."

As the stories wound down and people began to get ready to leave, her mother stood in the front of the room again.

This time, she looked right at Morgan as she said, "Thank you all for joining me in saying goodbye to an incredible man. I hope you all remember that even if someone you love isn't with you, they still love you, just as you love them. But sometimes love means letting go."

Annabelle came and stood next to Morgan. Flamboyant, even at a wake, she wore her autumn-orange dress, one that she said was a favorite of Auggie's. Her bleached-blond hair was pulled back in an almost neat bun, but frantic little curls were trying to make their escape.

Her mother leaned over and whispered, "And sometimes love means asking someone to come back."

That Annabelle wanted Morgan to come home to the Pittsburgh, Pennsylvania, neighborhood she'd grown up in was no secret. But neither were Morgan's reasons for not obliging her mom. She scanned the crowd for the two biggest reasons, but didn't see them. They must have left. For the first time today she breathed a sigh of relief.

"You have to let it go, Mom. I love the life I've built. It's what I want."

"Honey, sometimes what you think you want isn't what you want at all."

Morgan knew that she didn't want to be here in Pennsylvania. She wanted her life in San Diego, California. Where the weather was temperate and the ocean was a short car ride away. She wanted her job and career advancement. She was up for a big promotion, so that was all on track. Things with her on-again, off-again boyfriend, Marvin, were on again and stronger than ever. She had good friends…a good life there.

That's what she wanted.

That's what she was going to have.

CHAPTER ONE

E.J., home may be where the heart is...but that doesn't mean the rest of me needs to be there as well, does it?

MORGAN ELISABETH MILLER KNEW she should be in San Diego, the recipient of that big promotion, an adoring boyfriend and all her friends at her side. Yes, she should be there with her wonderful life laid out ahead of her.

And that's just where she'd been two weeks ago, on the cusp of seeing all her plans and aspirations come to fruition.

Which made the fact that she was back home in Pittsburgh again six months after Uncle Auggie's funeral, tooling around town in her mother's snazzy-looking, red Mustang convertible, more than just a small detour in her plan...it was a pothole. More than that, it was a chasm.

Oh, hell, it was the whole freakin' Grand Canyon. On one side stood the life she'd wanted, worked and planned so hard for. On the other side was Pittsburgh and this.

She sighed. She didn't know how to bridge what she wanted and what she had.

And as much as Morgan loved her mother, she also missed having a whole country between them. Annabelle was…well, Annabelle.

"Hold on," her mother cried. "I want to show you just what this car can do."

"It can get us there in one piece," Morgan called out loudly. *Loudly* was the only level of speech that worked. With the top down and the radio blaring, even that was iffy.

Her mother punched the accelerator and the car sped down the highway.

"Mom!"

There was nothing Morgan could do but hold on and pray that they arrived at their destination in one piece.

When she was in a generous mood, she described her mom as unique and one of a kind. When she wasn't feeling quite so complimentary, she described her mother as crazy and eccentric.

Which description she used didn't really matter. Either way, Annabelle marched to the beat of her own drum and encouraged others—especially Morgan—to join in and live to that offbeat rhythm as well.

Her mother never understood that Morgan preferred a more traditional—normal—cadence to her life.

Morgan Miller liked knowing what was coming around the next bend. She lived by plans and lists. Although recently all her planning and list making had been shot to hell by a corporate decision to cut costs by downsizing the company.

She wasn't prepared for Jeremiah, the Napoleon-complex tyrant-in-the-making, calling her into his office and instead of offering her the promotion she'd been anticipating, telling her she'd been downsized.

A severance package—no matter how sweet it was— wasn't on her career path list.

When she'd graduated from UCLA with her M.B.A. and taken the job at LM Co., Morgan had thought she had it made—that all those little initials represented her big and shining future.

Now she'd taken a step backward and landed squarely where she'd begun in Pittsburgh, Pennsylvania. Ever since Uncle Auggie's funeral six months ago, her mother had been campaigning for Morgan to move home, which meant at least someone was happy about the current situation.

"Almost there," Annabelle said cheerfully over the music from her booming stereo.

They turned a corner and had no problem spotting which house the reception they were attending was at. Annabelle eased the Mustang in front of a huge brick home deep in the heart of Upper St. Clair. Cars lined the street; white tents could be seen in the back. And as soon as Annabelle turned off the stereo, tasteful music could be heard at a more comfortable decibel.

Squirrel Hill, where Morgan grew up, was a beautiful section of Pittsburgh. Upper St. Clair, just south of the city, was a newer, more moneyed sort of beautiful.

"Wow," she managed to gasp. "So this is how the other half lives."

She tried to smooth her light brown hair back into some semblance of a style as a valet approached and offered to park the car. She glanced at her mother's bleach-blond hair, which still looked perfect despite its slightly windblown state.

It just figured. Annabelle looked good no matter what.

Morgan managed to slither out of the seat without exposing herself, but it was a near thing. The bright yellow dress her mom had insisted she borrow was shorter than anything she owned.

Her mother assured her she looked beautiful.

Morgan didn't feel beautiful, she felt…drafty.

"Whose wedding is this?" she asked her mom.

"Penny and Sam's."

"And you're sure they won't mind my tagging along?"

"These society weddings are always so packed that I'm sure they won't even notice. Plus we're getting here late, so dinner's already been served. We're just in time for the dancing. One more guest on the dance floor won't make a difference."

Morgan had never been overly fond of dancing herself. It had to do with an awareness that she had no sense of rhythm. None at all. Not the slightest iota of timing.

So she didn't dance much if she could help it, and would have turned down her mother's offer if she hadn't spent the two weeks since she'd been home holed up in Uncle Auggie's house, trying to find a way to get her life back. When her mother had called today, she was so relieved to be out of the house that she wasn't going to mind if her mother tripped the light fantastic all night. She'd just sit back and enjoy watching her.

Her mom tugged on her attractive red dress. Morgan

wished she could follow suit, but her loaner dress was strapless. She was afraid too much tugging wouldn't be such a good idea.

"Do I look okay?" Annabelle asked, patting her hair.

"You look great," she exclaimed, meaning it.

Her mother smiled and said, "So do you. I knew that yellow would suit your complexion. It makes you look even tanner, and really brings out the carmel highlights in your hair. It never looked quite right on me."

Morgan resisted snorting at the statement. She'd yet to see her mother in anything that didn't look more than right on her.

Annabelle was the type of woman who could wear a grungy sweatsuit and make it look good.

"So let's go," she said.

They followed a brick walkway to the back of the house. The huge white tent they'd seen from the front stood dead center in the spacious, well-manicured yard. The gauzy fabric was drawn back in graceful swags, revealing the sea of white within. Tables covered with snowy-white tableclothes. Lily centerpieces.

The bride and groom stood inside the entryway, and Annabelle steered Morgan right toward them.

"Penny, Sam, we just wanted to say congratulations. I hope you have many happy years together," she said, hugging them both. "And Penny, you look just as lovely as I knew you would."

She turned and nodded at Morgan. "You remember my daughter, Morgan."

"Congratulations to you both," Morgan said on cue as she shook their hands. The couple smiled, but she caught the questioning look they threw each other before she and Annabelle turned and moved into the crowd.

"You never said how you know them," Morgan commented.

Her mother's attention was suddenly riveted on something across the tent.

"Mom?" Morgan said, sensing something was hinky. "How do you know Penny and Sam?"

"Well..." she drew out the word as far as she could, then admitted, "technically, I don't."

"Pardon?"

"I saw their invoice at the shop. It was Sunny's account, so normally I wouldn't have noticed it, but now that I'm boss—" her mother gave a not-so-happy sigh "—I have to go through everything, and this one happened to be in my hand when you called."

When August Banyon had passed away in the spring, he'd bequeathed his house to Morgan and his business to Annabelle. His wife had died years before, and they were really all the family he had left.

Annabelle had worked for him for more than thirty years at Oakland Chair and Dish Rental. Now she owned it.

She didn't sound as if making the adjustment from employee to owner was going very smoothly.

But at the moment Morgan wasn't particularly worried about the smoothness of the transition.

"And?" she prompted.

"Like I said, I was holding the invoice for this reception, getting ready to file it, when you called and said you'd finished your résumé and had mailed off a bunch of copies. You said you were bored, so I thought—"

"You thought I'd enjoy—" she leaned closer and dropped her voice to a stage whisper "—crashing a party?"

Annabelle looked nervous. Morgan knew that she'd known all along there was no way Morgan would have willingly gone to a reception uninvited.

"Mom, I don't do things like this. Let's go before someone catches on that we're party crashers."

Her mother gave a little wave of her hand. "Oh, get over yourself. I never could figure out how I ended up with such a stick-in-the-mud for a daughter."

"Annabelle," Morgan said in her best I-mean-business tone. She only called her by her first name when her mom was out of control. In Morgan's book, crashing a reception was way out of control. "Let's go."

"No. I want to dance and this is the place to do it."

"Mom, you can't just go crashing parties in order to dance."

"Sure I can. Why, where would you be if I hadn't crashed a party the night I met your father?"

"What?" Morgan hoped she'd heard wrong, or that she'd simply misunderstood.

She'd never given much thought to how her mother and father had met. Growing up, she wouldn't have asked, because she couldn't imagine her mother without her father, and vice versa. And once he was gone, talking about him seemed to cause her mother pain, so there had been very little reminiscing before Morgan moved to San Diego.

"Didn't I ever tell you that story?" Annabelle asked. She shook her head.

"Your father and I met here in Upper St. Clair just

over thirty years ago. He was best man for your uncle Nelson, and I came with a group of friends—"

Morgan realized with a sinking heart that she could fill in the rest of this sentence herself, so she interrupted. "Because you worked at the Chair and Dish Rental and knew where all the best receptions were."

"Exactly." Her mother had a wistful, faraway look as she continued. "We crashed parties a couple times a month. It was cheaper than hitting the bars, and to be honest, the quality of men we met was much better at receptions."

Annabelle smiled. "That night, I walked into a tent very much like this one and spotted your dad. He looked so handsome in his tux. And before I knew it, I'd introduced myself and asked him to dance."

It figured her mother was the one to do the asking. Morgan had never worked up enough nerve to be the asker rather than the askee.

"They were playing 'Moon River' when we stepped onto the floor. I'd danced with a lot of men, but I'd never felt anything like I did when your father took me into his arms. The tent smelled like lilacs. It was May, so it was chilly. It must have been going on ten at night, and after that first song, we drifted out of the tent and spent the rest of the evening dancing under the stars." She sighed.

For a moment, Morgan thought she saw tears in her mother's eyes, but a second later Annabelle was smiling again. "So you never know what's going to happen. Stop being a worrywart and go enjoy yourself."

"But what if they find out?"

"We've already introduced ourselves, honey. I guarantee who we are doesn't concern them a bit. They're wondering how much longer they have to stay before they can say good-night and be on their way to a brand-new life. So have fun."

"But—"

Her mother just gave a quick wink and hurried to the other side of the tent and the dance floor.

Now what was she going to do? Morgan wondered. She'd known coming home would be a mistake.

The only time she'd been home in the last five years was for Uncle Auggie's funeral six months ago, and that hadn't gone well. Although maybe funerals, by definition, weren't supposed to.

But in her wildest dreams, Morgan could never have imagined that coming home to Pittsburgh would turn her into a party crasher.

An inadvertent one, but a party crasher nonetheless.

Morgan wandered off toward what appeared to be a quiet corner. She'd just hide until her mother was ready to go.

This was her last party with her mom, she decided as she took a seat. She didn't care how bored she was in the future. She'd never trust a night's activities to Annabelle. When they went out next, she'd make the arrangements herself.

Morgan watched the bride and groom, both looking so happy as they whirled around on the dance floor. They were ready to face a bright and shiny future together. Morgan couldn't help but reflect on how her own particular future was so very uncertain.

She was living in the house she'd inherited from Uncle Auggie, with only his two lurking cats and his rather geriatric dog.

She had no job, no significant other and no immediate plans.

This wasn't in her five-year goals.

Morgan sighed.

"I hope that was a happy sigh," an unfamiliar, deep voice said.

She turned and found an übermasculine man standing behind her. A Southern-belle-swoon-worthy sort of man.

Dark hair, dark eyes, dark complection, killer smile. He was close enough that she could catch the faintest whiff of cologne, and added *smells good* to her mental list of macho-boy's characteristics. He was dressed all in black, and rather than look sinister, it just made him look striking. Handsome even.

"So what's a woman like you doing lurking in a dark corner?" he asked.

"Just enjoying the sights." The most enjoyable one happened to be the man in front of her.

"Conner Danning," he said, extending his hand.

Morgan took it and found her fingers enveloped by his much larger, warm ones. "Ah... Morgan Miller," she said.

It took a great deal of effort and thought to remember her name. One would think after introducing herself to people for over twenty-six years it would be easy, but as she stared at the man, this Conner Danning, there wasn't much room in her mind for more than thoughts of him.

Thoughts that centered around him being naked in bed...with her.

Naked in bed for a long, hot, sweaty time.

Morgan realized her hand was still in his and she tried to withdraw it, but not only was she thinking with a muddy, befuddled mind, it seemed that she was moving through mud as well. Her hand slid from his with agonizing slowness.

"Enjoying the sights, eh?" he asked, grinning.

She realized that she might have let go of his hand, but she hadn't let go of the sight of him. She was staring.

She averted her eyes for a moment, but they were irresistibly drawn back to him.

What would Annabelle do in this situation? The question was so absurdly out of character that for a moment Morgan forgot to be embarrassed. "The sights have greatly improved in the last few minutes."

CONNER HAD COME TO the back corner of the tent where he'd stored some of his equipment. He needed a fifth roll of film in order to capture yet another wedding in photographs.

Preserving history for posterity.

That's how he phrased what he did. It was also how he tried to make himself feel better about his job. And he needed to feel better about it because taking pictures at weddings wasn't quite what he'd planned to do as a career.

He knew he was feeling particularly dissatisfied today because he'd recently heard from his buddy, Luke. Luke was in Sri Lanka working on a spread for *National Geographic,* taking the kind of pictures that Conner had always dreamed of taking.

Taking pictures of exotic locales was far more in line with Conner's once-upon-a-time aspirations than taking pictures of the Petersons and the Joneses.

Yes, Luke's call had more than likely led to Conner's

current funk. But running into this brunette in the corner lightened his mood considerably.

Maybe his luck was changing.

At first she'd seemed a bit reticent, but as she shot him her feisty little "improved sights" comment, he realized she wasn't.

"Funny, I was about to say the same thing. I mean, about the sights improving."

"So what's a guy like you doing lurking in a dark corner, Conner?" she asked, a smile playing at the edges of her lips.

Lips he'd like to taste.

For the last two years he'd had little time for women. His life had been full to the point of overwhelming him without adding a woman to the mix. Though he had to admit, his monklike existence left a lot to be desired.

He'd almost forgotten what it was like to feel instant chemistry with the opposite sex until he shook Morgan Miller's hand.

He opened his bag, took out a roll of film and held it aloft. "I needed to reload."

"Professional photographer, or just a friend of the happy couple?"

"Professional." The designation felt rather false.

Okay, wedding photographer wasn't the type of professional designation he'd dreamed of. And to be honest, he hadn't really wanted *National Geographic* jobs like Luke's, either, although that job was closer than what Conner was doing.

No, what he'd dreamed about was a hard-hitting type of photojournalism that would take him around the world capturing important events as they happened.

He'd almost made it.

Instead, circumstances had led him elsewhere, and the only events he was capturing were the ones organized for happy couples in the greater Pittsburgh area.

Maybe coming to the realization that life sometimes just happened was what separated grown-ups from their childhood.

Life unfolds in its own way.

There was no way to direct its course. And Conner had learned all he could do was try and stay afloat.

That's about all he'd managed the last few years—staying afloat. But things were looking up. Maybe he could do more than tread water soon.

But soon wasn't now. So as much as he'd like to see this woman again, he'd best let it go. He didn't need any more complications.

"Well, I'd better get back to it," he said, feeling a stab of regret.

Morgan watched as Conner Danning popped his film into the camera. Before she had a chance to duck-and-cover, he'd snapped a couple pictures of her.

"Hey."

"Just making sure it was loaded correctly." He started toward the dance floor. "Nice meeting you, Morgan. Enjoy the wedding."

"You, too, Conner." *Say something else,* Morgan commanded herself.

Stop him.

Here was a man who sparked something in her that had been missing for a long time.

Lust. Pure and simple.

She wanted him.

But as much as she'd like to be straightforward and tell him so, it just wasn't in her. What she needed was an excuse. Even that was a stretch, so she did what her adventurous, party crashing mother would do, and called out, "Mr. Danning. Conner."

She wasn't sure what to say after that. Maybe he hadn't heard her and would just keep on walking?

But he had heard her and he didn't keep on walking. Instead, he turned and looked at her questioningly. "Yes?"

Think.

Think.

Think! she commanded herself.

"Any chance you'd consider getting some coffee with me sometime?"

If she were being forthright she'd explain she'd like to meet with him because she'd love a chance to jump his bones. That she'd like to buy the newest issue of *Cosmo* and try out all fifty of their ways-to-please-in-bed tips on him. That she'd like to see if it really was possible to spend a whole day in bed.

"I'm doing some, uh, local business research about the area and would like to pick your brain."

Okay, to be honest, his brains weren't what she wanted. But it sounded better than explaining what she *was* after.

"I'll treat," she added with a grin. Her move wasn't nearly as bold as her mother might have managed, but still, Morgan was proud of herself.

For a minute, he looked as if he was going to say no. He gave just the barest shake of his head.

She felt a stab of regret. Her ex, Marvin, had been nice on occasion, a pain on occasion, but during their off-again, on-again relationship he'd never ignited the heat in her that Conner Danning had in just these few brief minutes.

She swallowed her disappointment and said, "Never mind. That's all right."

He reached into his back pocket and handed her a business card. "I'd love to. Call me and we'll set something up for next week."

"Great," she said. "I'll look forward to it."

He had a sort of puzzled expression, but it cleared and he smiled before he walked into the crowd of wedding guests.

Morgan felt a bit giddy.

She was going to see him again.

Of course, now she had to think of some sort of business research he could help her with.

Business? Where had that come from?

Monkey business, maybe. But *business?*

She was going to have to scramble to come up with something.

"There you are," Annabelle said. "Since you're hiding in the corner, I'm going to guess you're ready to go."

"If you are."

"Oh, I'm more than ready. There wasn't one eligible man my age at this party. It's not that I wouldn't consider dating a younger man, but these were all practically children. And since you're sitting here alone, I'm going to guess you didn't have any better luck."

Morgan thought about telling her mom that she had indeed met a man, but quickly decided not to. She had no idea what Annabelle would do if she knew. She'd probably try to help, and thinking of all the ways that could go wrong silenced Morgan in a hurry.

"Mom, about crashing future receptions…"

"Don't worry. My reception crashing days are over. Wedding receptions aren't what they used to be," her mother grumbled as they retraced their route toward the front of the house.

Morgan didn't say it, but she sort of thought party crashing was a bigger success than she'd ever anticipated.

Her impromptu trip home was suddenly looking much more interesting.

CHAPTER TWO

E.J., haven't heard from you yet. Of course, you know that. You must still be in the wilds of South America performing your medical miracles. Have I mentioned lately that I admire your volunteering for Doctors International? Don't let it go to your head...you're still the same doofus whose idea of a good time is torturing his interns with that silly Frankenstein practical joke. You're a sick, sick man. I guess that's why we get along so well. LOL

Mom was definitely up to her old tricks yesterday. She turned me into a party crasher....

NOISE.
Incessant.
High-pitched.

Morgan's sleep-befuddled mind tried to pinpoint what it was.

Whatever the noise was, it was too much to sleep through, even for someone who was becoming more and more familiar with the concept of sleeping in.

Morgan's trip to Pittsburgh had at least given her that new skill. In fact, she'd discovered the hitherto unknown joy of late-night television, and developed a huge crush on Jon Stewart. And old movies. Spencer Tracy was her guy, which surprised her. He wasn't the type of man who attracted her in real life, but put him in a black-and-white film opposite Katherine Hepburn and Morgan got all warm and fuzzy over him.

The noise was interrupting her cute guy fantasies.

She whacked at the alarm clock, but that didn't quiet things down at all. Slowly, she woke up enough to realize that the noise wasn't from the clock, but rather from the phone.

Her eyes felt gritty as she opened them, thoroughly intending to glare at the offending device. But instead of looking at the nightstand, she found herself staring at Gilligan, her uncle's aging bulldog. And the view she had was definitely not his finest.

"Get down, Gilligan."

The dog turned around and gave her a long, lazy look, then flopped down on the bed, not budging so much as an inch from his original position.

Morgan reached around the overweight beast and picked up the phone.

"Hello?" Though her vision was still a bit sleep-fuzzed, she was pretty sure the clock next to the phone read eight thirty-six.

Eight thirty-six?

Whoever this was had best have a good excuse for calling this early on a Sunday. The reason had better involve at least the possibility of hospitalization, because nothing less would save them.

"Morgan, it's Sunny."

"Sunny?" she croaked as she stared at the clock again.

She'd known that news of her homecoming would get out, but didn't expect welcome-home calls quite so early in the morning. She did the math and realized how much earlier it was in San Diego, and felt even more exhausted.

"It's Sunday," Sunny said, way too perkily. "We thought you might like to meet us—"

"For brunch," Morgan stated. How could she have forgotten Sunday morning brunches at the diner? Then she remembered who else came to the brunches and said, "I don't think it would be wise—"

"She won't be there," Sunny said quickly, still able to read Morgan's thoughts after all these years. "Just me, Tessa and Nikki. We'd love to see you and have a chance to catch up."

"I'd love to see you all as well."

"Great. In about an hour and a half, then."

Morgan hung up and snuggled into the pillow, trying to collect her rather tenuous wits.

She hadn't been lying. She did want to see the old gang. But…

That *but* was followed by others.

Buts that had made it easier to leave Pittsburgh for San Diego. To leave all her history behind.

Yet here she was, back home, with nowhere to hide.

She punched her pillow and noticed that Gilligan

was standing on the floor, his pelvis wiggling. The poor old dog had been a terror in his younger years. He'd humped everything and anything. But Morgan suspected he'd developed doggy arthritis due to his advanced age. Now all he did for the most part was wiggle his pelvis. Part of her felt sad for the old dog, who was now deprived of his favorite pastime.

"Want out?" she asked.

He stopped midwiggle and barked. He sounded as if he were a lifetime smoker, his bark was so raspy and wheezy.

Morgan eased herself out of bed, let Gilligan into the backyard, then padded into the master bathroom. The black-and-white tiles and huge, cast-iron, claw-foot tub made it an inviting space, unlike a few of the other antique-stuffed rooms in the house. But even those had potential. Though she was going to put the house on the market, Morgan found herself itching to do a bit of redecorating.

She hoped she wouldn't be in Pittsburgh long enough to have time to indulge that whim.

She made short order of dressing, then took Uncle Auggie's vintage black BMW to the diner. It was so hard to believe it had been years since she'd gone to a Sunday brunch. The weekly meal with her friends used to be such an important part of her life, and now years had drifted by without her seeing them.

Oh, Morgan had seen Sunny at the funeral six months ago, because she worked at Uncle Auggie's store, Oakland Chair and Dish Rental. But Tessa and Nicole hadn't known him, other than in passing, and hadn't been there.

Unfortunately, Morgan's louse of an ex-fiancé had known Uncle Auggie and had felt the need to pay his respects. Thomas had worked at OCDR throughout college and she knew he'd liked the older man.

That's how Morgan had met him.

She'd gone into the store to visit her mother one day, and there he was. Tall, beach-boy blond and beyond gorgeous. At two years her senior, he'd been the older boy that every girl dreamed about.

And by *every,* she meant herself and Gina, her ex-best friend, the skanky fiancé stealer.

Morgan remembered the day Thomas and Gina had broken the news to her. She'd thought it was wonderful, her fiancé and her best friend giving her a surprise evening out so they could all plan the wedding together. Instead of a happy wedding-planning dinner, Thomas and Gina had sat her down and explained that they'd fallen in love.

That was the last time Morgan had talked to either of them.

After they'd declared their undying love for each other and apologized to her, she'd simply got up from the table and walked out.

Within weeks, she'd packed up and moved to California. She'd worked at a Starbucks and applied to grad school. She'd been accepted at UCLA, where she finished her degree.

She thought she'd moved on.

But here she was, in Pittsburgh, parking the car and heading to a Sunday morning brunch with the old gang and wondering if she'd ever really moved at all.

She asked herself the question again as she reached the

door of the small restaurant they had gathered at every Sunday morning in the past. The Fifth Avenue Diner was one of those places that always stayed the same.

The green awning might have faded from a dark hunter shade to a fall-grass hue, and there might be a few more cracks in the sidewalk, but otherwise, it looked as it had in her college days.

Morgan opened the door and walked in. There was still a board to the left with the day's specials listed, and the tables were arranged exactly as she remembered them.

She walked toward the far corner table, where two women were sitting. Before she joined them, Morgan stood a moment, staring at her friends, enjoying the wave of nostalgia. She'd missed this connection. She hadn't realized how much until this very moment.

She cleared her throat and the woman with her back toward her turned, the one in the corner looked up.

"Geez, Nikki, tough night?" Morgan asked the sunglasses-wearing brunette.

Nicole Hastings pushed the glasses up, revealing eyes alight with warmth and recognition. She plopped the glasses back into place and sprang to her feet even as Sunny squealed, "Morgan!"

Morgan saw Nikki wince at the sound, but couldn't help a small squeal of her own as they all three hugged.

"Where's Tessa?" she asked, as they settled at the large round table. She took her seat between Nikki and Sunny without even thinking. It was *her* seat, and she knew that even when she wasn't home, it was there, waiting for her. Just as Tess's seat was empty now. Waiting.

And then there was Gina's....

Morgan refused to let thoughts of her ex-friend spoil the reunion.

"Tess is always late, if she comes at all," Sunny Paterniti said. Blond, stunning, but more rounded since their college days, Sunny took Morgan's hand, giving it a squeeze. "She'd have been here if she'd known you were home. I just found out myself yesterday, when your mom mentioned it. Normally, I'd have known the minute you arrived, but Annabelle hasn't been herself since she took over running the store. She's spending so much time in the back office we don't get to chat like we normally do."

"How long are you here for?" Nikki asked.

"I'm here indefinitely," Morgan admitted.

"Staying with Annabelle?" Nikki asked.

"No. Uncle Auggie left me his house. Living right next door to Mom is about as close as I can manage. I thought I'd just have Mom sell it, but she's been swamped at the Chair and Dish Rental and hadn't gotten to it yet. I guess it was for the best. I'm able to use it now while I look for a new job."

"So what happened?" Nikki asked.

Morgan gave them an abbreviated version of her laid-off, looking for a new job but not a new love spiel.

Their commiseration over her downsizing and breakup with Marvin felt like a balm, soothing small hurts she hadn't even known she was nursing.

"So fill me in on what's going on with both of you," she said, not wanting to talk about the life in San Diego that she'd lost—the life she was determined to get back.

Sunny dug in her purse and pulled out a wallet.

"Johnny's almost a year now and brilliant, if I do say so myself."

"And you can be sure she'll say so again and again," Nikki teased.

"Hey, I can't help it if my kid's a genius. He's already saying Mama."

Morgan wasn't sure saying Mama constituted brilliant, but she didn't say so. "Most babies can't talk at this age?"

"Not before their first birthday, but Johnny's brilliant, remember?" Nikki grinned as Sunny shot her a mama-bear look.

"I can't wait until you get to know him. He's just going to love his auntie Morgan." Sunny launched into a momfest monologue, but Morgan thought what she wasn't saying was the most telling.

She talked about her son, about her job, about her friends.

Sunny wasn't saying a word about a man in her life. To the best of Morgan's knowledge, there hadn't been so much as a date since Johnny's father had walked out on her.

Sunny seemed as bright and chipper as normal, but Morgan listened for some hint of sadness. If there was any, her friend covered it well. Was she still pining over Johnny's father, the jerk who'd left her without so much as a backward glance?

Morgan decided not to beat around the bush. "So, any men in your life?"

"No, no men. I'm not looking. Between Oakland CDR and Johnny, I don't have the time or the inclination."

"The day I stop *inclining* is the day you can pull the plug," Nikki vowed. "And don't even get me started on Sunny's wasting her education at the Chair and Dish Rental."

Nikki picked up the threads of the old argument, and again Morgan was hit with a sense that nothing had changed in the last five years.

Except for maybe Morgan herself.

She felt like a square peg trying to fit back into a round hole.

"Actually, it is a great use of my education," Sunny corrected, glaring at Nikki.

Okay, maybe not everything had stayed the same.

Back in the old days, Sunny hadn't become ruffled.

And glaring?

It just hadn't been in her nature.

But somewhere over the last few years, Sunny had obviously toughened. And Morgan had missed her metamorphosis.

What else had she missed?

Before she could ask more questions and try to find out, Nikki said, "Nothing much has changed with me, either."

"Except for men." Sunny used a teasing tone, but there was a hint of retaliation in what she said. "A new one every week, that's our Nik."

Nikki didn't seem to take offense. She just grinned. "Hey, I figure, statistically, my chances of finding Mr. Right are better if I play the field."

"But you'll never know if a man could be right unless you stick around for more than a date or two," Sunny said.

"I'll know the right one when I find him. And I guarantee he wasn't last night's date. The man still lives with his mother and proudly admitted he'd never done his own laundry. Not ever. He's in his thirties."

Before Nikki could go off on one of her man dia-
tribes, Morgan asked, "How about work?"

"I'm still writing my column for the paper." Nikki
had interned at the *Pittsburgh Press* while they were still
in college. "That's what last night was really about—
next week's column. It's on Pittsburgh's newest hot spot,
aptly enough named Hot Spot. It's in the strip district.
And let me tell you, they make a mean apple martini."

Sunny turned the tables on Morgan by asking, "So,
what have you been doing since you got back? Because
you obviously haven't been calling us. We still wouldn't
have known you were home if Annabelle hadn't finally
mentioned it at work yesterday."

"I was going to call as soon as I had things in order."

"You're still an order freak, eh?" Nikki asked. "Bet
you have a list."

"Lists, heavy emphasis on the plural," Sunny added.

"Maybe a small list. The first week was filled with
the move and trying to get nominally settled. This last
week, I wrote a killer résumé, sent it out, walked the
dog…and crashed a party."

She'd known that would get them.

Sunny pounced on it first. "Crashed a party? That
doesn't sound like you."

"No, but it does sound like my mom's idea of a good
time." She filled them in on Penny and Sam's reception,
and meeting Conner Danning, ending with, "So I asked
him out. Said I wanted to pick his brain about business."

"Oh, you've done me proud," Nikki gushed. "So
what excuse are you going to give him?"

"I thought I'd use the family business. Okay, it's
really just become the family business, and it's Mom's

rather than mine, but still, she's family, so it's not a big lie. I thought I'd tell him I was thinking of expanding beyond just chairs and dishes into renting other wedding and party supplies. That gives me an excuse for wanting to go to other receptions with him so I can gather ideas."

"Why didn't you just ask if he'd be interested in being your boy toy while you're home?" Nikki asked. "I mean, I've discovered most men don't mind a bit of noncommitment fun."

"Most men prefer it," Sunny said softly.

Morgan would like to hunt down Sunny's ex for putting that thread of pain into her friend's voice.

"I wouldn't know how to propose boy toying," she confessed. "I've been dating Marvin for so long, I'm not sure I remember how to start a new relationship, even a casual one."

"You've been *not* dating Marvin for just as long as you've been dating him," Nikki said with a grin.

"So we had a tumultuous relationship."

"Had?" Sunny asked. "As in, it's off again?"

"For good this time," Morgan said. "It should have been off for good soon after we started dating, but he was comfortable. I mean, he drove me crazy, but there's truth to the devil-you-know theory."

"So, rather than come right out and tell this photographer you're in town just long enough to get a new job, and are looking for a good bone-jumping while you're here, you're going to follow him around and pretend to do research you don't need to do?" Nikki asked.

"When you put it like that it doesn't sound like such a great idea, does it? But really, researching new avenues for the business is a great idea. Oakland Chair and Dish Rental has always brought in a living, but there have to be other, untapped rental opportunities. I'm going to head over to the store tomorrow and see what's changed and then maybe find some ways for my mother to make a difference."

"I still think you should just tell this guy you want him," Nikki said good-naturedly. "After all, when you pick up a guy while crashing a party, you can tell him anything you want."

What did she want?

Morgan didn't think she wanted to just jump his bones, regardless of the fact he sparked for her.

What she wanted was to get out of Pittsburgh and head back to San Diego and a new job.

Actually, what she wanted was to go back to her old life there, and she knew that wasn't going to happen.

Things were changing.

And she didn't like it at all.

"You know," Nikki said slowly, "party crashing… that's not such a bad idea. The bar scene is getting more than a little old."

"I'm not crashing anything," Sunny blurted.

"And it could be a fun column for the paper," Nikki continued. "Party Crashing…the New Dating Scene?" Morgan could practically see her brain at work as she murmured, "You know, that's not bad."

"What's not bad?" a new voice asked.

Everyone turned toward Tessa, a statuesque woman sporting designer slacks, a soft cream colored blouse and a much shorter haircut than in the past. It took her a moment to spot Morgan. When she did there was a new wave of shrieking and hugging.

"Come on, you guys," Nikki muttered, despite the fact she'd been in the thick of the hugging. "The problem with having women friends is their voices are high enough not to be very sympathetic to hangover victims."

"You did it to yourself," Tess said, taking her seat. "That means you're no victim and as such don't get any sympathy."

"And here I was, about to ask you out on a little adventure," Nikki informed her.

They all talked at once, filling in each other's sentences as they caught Tessa up on why Morgan was home and the idea Nikki had for her newest article.

Morgan listened, smiling, the knowledge that she was well and truly home finally sinking in. She might want to get back to her life in San Diego, but she'd been right—her heart was here in Pittsburgh.

CHAPTER THREE

E.J., I've been reading books, trying to find myself. Currently, I'm reading Jon Kabat-Zinn's *Wherever You Go, There You Are*. It hasn't answered my burning question, how did I get here, and how do I get out?

ON MONDAY, FEELING AS IF she was indeed sliding down a rabbit hole into chaos, Morgan tried to figure out how to get back in control.

Returning to Pittsburgh temporarily had been quite an adjustment. Morgan actually slept in until nine one morning, and she hadn't walked once since she'd arrived. When she did exercise, it mainly consisted of hurrying toward a table where a waiter would bring her coffee and a pastry.

Worst of all, she felt she'd lost sight of her goals.

Morgan knew herself well enough to realize she

functioned better with a clearly defined plan. So she tried to lay it out in her mind. For starters, she wanted to be home in San Diego before E.J. got back from his current stint abroad.

She was right on track for that. She'd sent out a million résumés the previous week. Okay, not a million, but it felt like it. She'd used every contact she had to network her way into a new job.

Jeremiah, her old boss, had actually made a few calls on her behalf, and sent her some contacts who might be interested in a midlevel manager looking for an opportunity to advance.

So, goal number one—get a new job—was on track.

Goal number two…more than the new job and the new challenge, she wanted her old life back. Pittsburgh was all right for a visit—better than she'd thought it would be, actually—but she wouldn't want to live here forever.

With her mind racing, Morgan decided to start her day off by walking over to the store. While one short walk wouldn't fight off her jobless lassitude it was a few steps toward getting back to her old outlook.

Exercise. Work hard. Have well-defined goals.

So she walked.

Oakland Chair and Dish Rental was about twenty minutes away from the Squirrel Hill district. She thought about *really* jumping back into her life and jogging over, but didn't want to arrive all sweaty, so she settled for walking fast.

She'd made this exact trip almost daily when she was younger—through the hilly residential area of old brick homes, some with vinyl siding. Gradually some apartments appeared, and finally Forbes Avenue, with all its hustle and bustle.

She walked past Carnegie Mellon University, past the museum and finally past the cathedral. Morgan loved walking by the massive stone building, so tall and majestic. She used to bring her homework over to the grassy park in front of it and study in its shadow.

She thought about walking through for old times' sake, but decided to wait. Maybe she'd get some lunch later and come sit in its shadow once again.

Passing the cathedral, she arrived in front of Oakland Chair and Dish Rental.

It hadn't changed since those earlier days. Maybe it was a little shabbier. The sign in front could use updating, and a good coat of paint would do wonders for the exterior of the small office front on Forbes.

She wondered about the state of the huge warehouse a few blocks away on Oakland Avenue, which housed OCDR's supplies.

When Morgan opened the door, the bell chimed merrily in the empty reception area, which, she noted could use a touch of paint as well. Walls that had once been a bright white had faded to a muted ecru. The front counter was cluttered with display books and papers. The small seating area held odds and ends from the rental business, and three-year-old magazines.

She pulled a small book out of her purse and started to take notes, almost sighing with contentment. Another list… Yes, she was really getting back to normal.

Paint was the top priority. She walked behind the counter, looking for a computer, but didn't see one. Maybe it was in Uncle Auggie's office? Scratch that.

She had to start thinking of all this as her mom's. So, maybe it was in her *mother's* office? Wherever it was, Morgan would be willing to bet it was years out of date.

"Hi, honey." Annabelle came out of the back room, wearing a skintight green shirt that didn't do much for her complexion, but certainly emphasized her bra size. "I was going to call you this afternoon."

"Then I'm glad I stopped by. I wanted to check out the store." Morgan turned in a circle. "Nothing's changed."

Sunny emerged from the back room as well. "Ah, but I'm sure before the end of your stay you'll have a few suggestions, won't you? Maybe even a few ideas about how to expand the business?"

Morgan tucked the book into her open purse. "You know, that wouldn't be such a bad idea, *Susan.*" Using Sunny's real name had the intended effect.

Her friend's perpetual smile slipped a notch. "That's Sunny. I know you've been gone a long time, so I guess you've forgotten that I go by Sunny."

Her friend tried to glare, but it only made Morgan laugh. At the sound, Sunny relented and laughed with her. "Don't start with me, Morgan," she warned with mock ferocity.

"Wouldn't think of it, Sunny."

Annabelle interrupted the teasefest. "Come into the back, honey, would you?"

Morgan followed her into the office at the rear of the shop. The room had been neat as a pin when Uncle Auggie had been in charge. Annabelle obviously had a different business style. One that included quite a bit of chaos.

"I was going to call you about a business question. Well, not a question, but more of a favor." Her mother seemed uncharacteristically hesitant. "You see, I had a visit from a man who's interested in buying me out and I would like your input."

"Are you interested in selling?"

The thought of OCDR leaving the family hadn't occurred to Morgan. Now that her mother had brought up the possibility, she realized how very little she liked it.

She'd known for years that Uncle Auggie planned to hand over the store to her mom and Morgan had expected it to always be a part of her life, just as it always had been. She had grown up hanging out here; working at OCDR had been her first job. Her friends had visited here.

She'd met Thomas here, not that that was a great memory. Oh, meeting him was, but the pain of leaving him tainted her enjoyment of the others.

But good memories or bad ones, Oakland Chair and Dish Rental was part of home.

"I don't know if I could sell it," her mother said. "But I'm not sure I actually want to run it. I didn't think owning rather than just working here would make that much of a difference, but it does. I was content handling sales. Being in charge is so much more time consuming. And ultimately, every decision rests with me. I just don't know if I want to keep at it. What if I make a mistake and ruin a business Auggie spent his life building? If I sold the store, maybe I could keep working here for the new owner."

"I couldn't imagine anyone but Uncle Auggie or you running things here. A total stranger at the helm of OCDR?" Morgan shook her head. It just didn't feel right.

"I'm not saying I'll do it, but I thought it made sense

to check out the offer. I was hoping you'd do it for me. You know a lot more about business than I do."

"Mom, I don't know if I'm qualified to make this kind of decision for you."

"Not make the decision, just give me an opinion. I'm supposed to meet the man on Thursday. Maybe you could spend the next few days reacquainting yourself with the business. Then you'd be prepared."

"I—"

Her mother cut off her protest by simply asking, "Please? I know that ultimately I have to make the decision, but I would really value your opinion."

Morgan shrugged. "Sure. Why not? I'd wanted to take a look at things anyway, sort of for old times' sake. So why don't you show me the new computer system and I'll get started."

"What new computer system?" Her mother looked at her blankly.

"The one I talked to Uncle Auggie about two, almost three years ago? The one designed to streamline your filing and ordering systems. The one networked with the warehouse."

Her mother smiled and nodded. "Oh, that system."

"Yes. That one. If you could show me where you keep it, I'll get started." Morgan looked around the small, cluttered office, then back at her mom.

She didn't meet her eyes. "It's not here."

"Where is it?" Morgan asked. "At the warehouse?"

That wouldn't make sense. Having a component there made sense, but not the whole system.

"Well," Annabelle said slowly, "you see, Auggie didn't buy the computer. We both decided the old system has worked for the last forty years, so why change it."

"Nothing's been updated? You're still using the old method?" Paper files, index cards, no sense of order…

"You know the old saying, if it ain't broke, don't fix it? Well, we didn't see the need. Look, I have all the recent files right here for you." Her mother nodded at a teetering stack on the corner of the desk. "Want me to bring you something to drink while you go through them?"

"How 'bout a Scotch?" Morgan muttered.

"What, dear?"

She tried to force a smile. "A cup of coffee would be great."

"Sure thing. I can't thank you enough for helping. I know I have decisions to make, but it's wonderful to have someone who knows more about business lending me some insight…" Annabelle hurried out the door, and a few minutes later Sunny came back with the coffee.

Her friend gave Morgan a long, sympathetic look. "It's not as bad as it seems."

"This system is antiquated beyond belief. It's going to take me most of the week to sort through all this and come up with some comprehensive picture of where the business stands."

"If it makes you feel better, I lobbied both your mom and Auggie for the computer system. But they're both technophobes."

"I'd say let's invest in one now, but if Mom's selling…" She let the sentence trail off. "Are you okay with the idea of her selling?"

"Tess, Nikki and Gi…uh, well, they would say that

her selling and my losing this job would be the best thing that ever happened to me. I'd finally be forced to step outside my comfort zone."

Morgan decided to ignore Sunny bringing up Gina's name. Instead, she asked, "And you? What would you say?"

On the surface, Sunny would seem the most easy-going of their group, but Morgan had long since learned that her friend had a spine of steel when there was something she wanted, or didn't.

"I'd say that I like working here. I like the hours. I like that they let me bring Johnny in if I have to. Your mom's a hoot, and Auggie was the sweetest, most generous man I ever met. Did I tell you he set up a college fund for Johnny? Took out a life insurance policy when Johnny was born and put it in our names. It's left us financially set now."

"That sounds like Auggie." A neighbor and employer who, when he lost his wife, had built himself a family. Annabelle, Sunny, little Johnny… And Morgan knew she was on the list, despite the fact she'd left Pittsburgh years ago. Uncle Auggie had even visited her in San Diego, and she'd talked to him as often as she talked to her mother on the phone.

He had been her family.

They had all been his.

"So, to get back to your question," Sunny said, "I'd miss working here, but I'd be fine. Your mother has to do what's best for her."

"About this man who wants to buy the store? Did you meet him?"

Sunny just chuckled in a way that left Morgan feeling

a bit nervous. When she finally stopped, her huge grin was almost as disconcerting.

"What?"

"Nothing." Sunny batted her baby-blue eyes, the picture of innocence.

But Morgan knew her well enough not to buy the look, and glared at her, which only made Sunny laugh again.

"Really, nothing. He seemed businessy and to the point when he came in last week."

"And?"

"And…I don't know if you remember, but way back when, during one Sunday brunch, we all came up with our ideal man, yours was a businessman. Black hair, blue eyes. I think you described him as Remington Steele, M.B.A. not P.I. A well-cut and polished sort of man."

"How do you remember these things, Sunny?"

She shrugged and grinned. "It's a gift. Ask me something I should know, and I won't have a clue. But the minutia…it's stuck rock-solid in my brain. And the second this man walked in, I remembered that conversation and thought, there he is, Morgan's man. He has this deep, commanding sort of voice. Actually, if I had to describe the guy's aura, that would be it. Commanding. Demanding of attention."

"A demanding man isn't what I'm looking for."

"Maybe I'm not describing him well enough, because when you see him, he's your Pierce Brosnan dream guy with a touch of Trump incarnate."

Morgan laughed. "Pierce Brosnan meets Donald Trump? We'll see. Right now, I'm going to have to see if I can make heads or tails of this data."

"Holler if you need any help."

"I will."

Sunny left her with coffee in hand, a disorganized stack of files in front of her and a fantasy about her old dream guy playing in her head.

Suddenly, Morgan's quiet, boring time in Pittsburgh seemed a lot more lively. Making heads or tails of OCDR's records. Business meetings with Pierce. Pseudo business meetings with Conner, who definitely wasn't a clone of her Pierce fantasy. He was a scruffy photographer—a wonderful job, but not an M.B.A. sort of field. No, he wasn't the one, but he'd been the center of more than one lurid fantasy since they'd met.

Morgan was humming as she dived into the files and started compiling notes. This was what she thrived on— a busy, productive life.

She left the office at lunch to walk home and get her laptop. It might not have the business software she'd suggested OCDR buy, but she had a decent spreadsheet program to organize all the data.

When she opened the door, Gilligan lumbered into the hallway and seemed excited to see her. Well, excited in an aging bulldog, breathing-is-almost-too-much-energy-output way. He gave a wheezy yap of greeting.

Morgan knelt down to pat his head. She'd forgotten what it was like to have someone waiting at home to say hi. She and Marvin had never lived together, despite their long relationship. As a matter of fact, the thought had never occurred to her. She'd liked having her own space.

She grabbed a sandwich and let the dog out, then hurried right back to the office and dived in again, losing herself in the figures and information, feeling more and more at home by the minute.

"We're closing up," her mother said.

Morgan jerked her gaze from the computer screen to the clock. "It's five o'clock already?"

"When I asked you for help, I didn't mean you had to do this." Annabelle waved her hand, gesturing at the piles of paper. "I just wanted you to talk to Mr. Jameson."

"I can't tell you if his offer is a good one without knowing what the company's worth."

Her mother sighed. "Morgan, you worry too much. Whatever happens, it will be fine. Ultimately, the decision's mine. There's no right or wrong answer for you. I just want your impressions of Mr. Jameson and his proposal. Whatever happens after that I'm sure will be the right thing. Life has a way of going where it should."

"I guess therein lies our greatest difference. You're the glass half-full, and I'm—"

"The glass half-empty?"

"No. I'm the get-a-bottle-of-water-and-fill-the-stupid-thing-yourself kind of woman."

Her mother laughed and kissed her forehead. "Do you want to do dinner tonight? It's on me. After all, I'm not cutting you a paycheck for all the work you're doing." She paused. "Unless you need me to? I mean, do you—"

Morgan shook her head. "I'm fine financially, but thanks."

Annabelle nodded. "If that changes, you know you'd just have to tell me."

"I do. And I'll tell you what, I have about ten more minutes of work here, then a call to make. If you run home and let Gilligan out, I'll finish up before you're back, then dinner it is."

"It's a plan." Her mother hurried out of the office with a backward wave.

Rather than return to the data she was collating, Morgan pulled a business card from her pocket. She studied the number and picked up the phone, then set it back in place.

Conner Danning.

He definitely wasn't the Remington Steele meets Donald Trump sort of man she'd always lusted over. Despite the fact he'd had on nice clothes, it wasn't a suit and tie. He'd had five o'clock shadow in the middle of the afternoon, and his hair had needed a good stylist. And a photographer wasn't a high-powered business-man. It sounded like a precarious job at best.

No, Conner wasn't the kind of man she usually dated. Then again, Marvin had been *exactly* the kind of man she usually dated, and look how that had turned out!

Their relationship was lackluster when it was on, and almost a relief when it was off.

So maybe someone who wasn't exactly her type was just what she needed, despite the fact she was telling a little white lie in order to meet with him.

Feeling resolute, she picked up the phone and dialed.

He picked up on the first ring. "Hello?"

"Hi, Conner. This is Morgan Miller. We met at the reception this weekend. I wondered if we could get together...."

CHAPTER FOUR

ON THURSDAY AFTERNOON, AFTER Annabelle Miller had closed the store for the day, she studied herself in the mirror at home.

Not too bad, if she did say so herself.

And she did.

She'd never been a pretty girl. As she aged she'd decided handsome might be an appropriate description. But her looks had never stopped her from attracting the attention of men. She had a confidence that was instilled in her by her mother.

"Annabelle, honey," her mom would say in that soft Southern lilt. "Boys are simple creatures. You just be yourself, let what's in you shine, believe you're the most beautiful creature there is and that's just what they'll see—how very beautiful you are."

Annabelle had always tried to do just that, and it had worked.

Her husband, bless him and his not overly clear eyesight, not only didn't notice that she was simply handsome, he'd told her that when she'd walked into the reception she'd taken his breath away. He'd never seen anyone that beautiful.

Annabelle sniffed. She missed him, even after all these years. But she knew he'd be the first to tell her it was long past time to get on with her life and find someone else to love. Loving someone new wouldn't minimize the love she'd had for him.

She held up the red dress, then a bright yellow one, trying to decide what to wear.

The yellow one reminded her of Morgan.

Annabelle loved her daughter, but that wasn't so rare. Most mothers did.

She tossed the red dress down. Too here-I-am. And yellow was a color she kept buying, even though she knew it did nothing for her complexion.

She went back to rummaging through her closet, thinking of Morgan.

It wasn't just that she loved her daughter because she was her mom. Annabelle admired Morgan's tenacity, her single-mindedness—okay, it was more stubbornness than single-mindedness. And she loved Morgan's ability to organize things.

To be honest, now that she thought about it, she sometimes admired Morgan's stubbornness, and sometimes it just drove her crazy.

Take Morgan's ex-fiancé, Thomas, for instance.

Annabelle pulled out a brown dress, which was certainly more understated, and held it up, studying the effect in the mirror.

Dowdy.

Back to the closet.

She had tried to tell Morgan that Thomas wasn't the right man for her. He was her clone. A business-minded, organized sort of man. They would have bored each other to tears within a year of being married.

And that Marvin in California? Well, at least they fought now and again—that type of friction was probably what had kept their relationship going so long. But still, he was another button-down bore of a man.

She took a white dress that looked virginal until she held it up to herself. She smiled. Yes, this was the one. It had black trim, which meant it was proper…well, proper enough.

She slid it over her head and sat down to do her makeup.

Morgan might think that a business type like Thomas or Marvin was what she wanted, but Annabelle knew what her daughter needed. Someone to keep her on her toes. Someone who would fill in the gaps in her life and draw Morgan out of herself.

All that was why she hadn't planned to ask Morgan to talk to the potential buyer. B. Mark Jameson was a most decidedly button-down type of man. But after Sunny had let it slip that Morgan had a case of lust over some photographer she'd met at the wedding they crashed, Annabelle had reconsidered asking for Morgan's help.

If Morgan was already interested in another man, then it was probably safe to let her scope out Jameson's offer. Annabelle felt it was a good omen that Morgan had met the new interest while crashing a party.

Plus, a photographer wasn't a nine-to-fiver. If Morgan was interested in him, then maybe her tastes had changed. Which meant it was definitely okay to send her out with the wannabe buyer.

Annabelle surveyed her outfit in the mirror. Tasteful, refined and… She leaned forward and flashed the mirror a chestful of cleavage.

Hot.

Yes, the old girls were still her best feature. They did her proud in this dress.

She pirouetted one more time and glanced at her watch.

Morgan was with her photographer right now, then meeting the potential buyer for dinner. Which meant she'd never notice that her mother was slipping out.

Annabelle had promised Morgan she wouldn't crash any more receptions. But a blowout sixtieth birthday party certainly didn't count as a reception. It was a celebration.

And if she happened to celebrate along with a bunch of strangers, that wasn't really crashing, it was just being a warmhearted sort of person who wanted to share other people's joy.

If she happened to meet an eligible man there, and decided to celebrate with him, well…

Annabelle smiled and picked up her purse. She was ready.

CHAPTER FIVE

E.J., I like to think of myself as a very honest person, but a fib doesn't count as a real lie. Right? I mean, that's why they call it a fib, and not a lie...

WHEN MORGAN ARRIVED AT THE small Oakland coffeehouse and spotted Conner, she was pleased to discover it was still there—that electric sort of awareness she'd had when she met him at the reception.

She had wondered over the last few days if maybe she'd just imagined the spark between them. After all, she wasn't the type who fell head-over-heels in lust.

But there it was. Big, strong and practically pulsating as she slid into the chair across from him.

Although now that she *was* sitting across from him, she wasn't exactly sure what to do about it. Even if he did let her tag along to a few events, she wasn't sure she'd have the nerve to let him know that she wanted him.

Her mother would simply tell a man that she felt something, but Morgan couldn't bring herself to do that, so she settled for saying, "Hi. Thanks again for meeting with me."

She was glad she'd done her homework about the OCDR. She clutched the file as if it was some sort of talisman.

She still couldn't figure out what it was that attracted her to Conner. Today he had on well-worn jeans and a plain black T-shirt that hugged his chest. It didn't look as if he'd shaved, and he'd slung a ratty brown canvas shoulder bag across the next chair.

It definitely wasn't the *GQ* look Morgan normally went for, which was why she couldn't figure out what this attraction was based on. But it was there, leaving her feeling a bit breathless as she ad-libbed after the waitress had brought her a coffee.

"The store rents out the basics. Chairs, tables, dishes, cookware, glassware, silverware, table linens. But there are untapped party avenues. Take a wedding reception, for instance. What other merchandise could we offer to rent...or even sell? Everyone's so busy. Going to multiple stores can take up a lot of time. Why not offer everything in one place? A one-stop party destination."

"Your store has room and the capital to expand to carry a full line of party items?" Conner questioned.

"Maybe not. That's what I'm trying to decide—what we could carry and what we could afford to carry. Maybe we could simply work as middlemen. Rather than try to stock everything we'd need to sell—invitations, for instance—what if we worked with another local shop, carried their samples, allowed customers to shop with us, then turned the order over to the other store? We'd keep a percentage for having contracted the order. Or maybe it would be better to just do it ourselves. I don't know. That's where my proposal for you comes in."

"Ah, now that sounds intriguing," he said, chuckling. "You've got a proposal for me?"

Tingly.

She felt tingly all over at the sound of his laughter.

Marvin never made her feel that.

Annoyed, yes, but not particularly tingly—

She cut off the thought. Now, where was she?

Proposals. Ignoring the tingles, she continued, "Yes. I don't know how intriguing you'll find it. You're a photographer." She stopped and shook her head. "Like you didn't know that. Sorry. But given the nature of your work, you go places I need to research. I want to visit some other receptions. See what kind of items they use, and what ones OCDR could carry. I'd be your girl Friday. Help haul equipment. Whatever. I just want to scope out the parties."

"A free assistant. That's an offer I don't get very often." He smiled. "Okay, an offer I've never received."

The offer she wanted to make involved a lot of skin, a big bed and a long afternoon. But she didn't know how to go about making that type of suggestion without blushing or laughing…or both. So this was her next best option.

"So, what do you say?" she pressed.

"I say fine. I can't see how having an assistant could hurt anything. It would be fun."

"Great. So, when's your next booking?"

"Saturday." He took a business card out of his pocket and began to write, then handed it to her. "Why don't I pick you up and we'll ride out together."

Morgan glanced at the card, then stuffed it in her purse. She scribbled her address on a napkin. "That's great. What time?"

"It's a four o'clock wedding. So, about two? Photographing weddings is about more than just taking pictures at the ceremony and reception. Our day starts with photographing the bride getting ready, the groom, the attendants, and proceeds from there. It makes for a long day."

"That's fine. I'll see you then." She glanced at her watch.

"Do you have another appointment?" he asked.

"Yes." She wondered what to tell him, and opted for as much honesty as possible. "There's a local businessman interested in buying the store."

"So, you're selling or expanding?"

"Not me, my mom. And yes, she's weighing the possibilities. She's just not sure what she wants to do with the business."

"So when you're not brokering deals, and researching expansion for your mother's company, what do you do?"

"I was an account manager for LM Co. in San Diego until recently. They downsized the department, which is a nice way of saying I lost my job. So I'm home in Pittsburgh, settling my uncle's estate, helping out my mom and looking for a new job."

"Same field, or something altogether different?"

"I loved my life and want it back. Same type of job, back in California." The answer came easily, but she realized she'd never even questioned what she'd do next. She'd just blithely started applying to similar companies for similar jobs in southern California.

Why?

Losing her job meant she had a clean slate. She could go anywhere, do anything.

Did she really want to go back to her old job?

Of course she did, she told herself. But she felt a little niggle of doubt.

"The earthquakes don't bother you?" Conner teased.

"The snow doesn't bother you?" she countered, concentrating on the man across from her and tabling questions about her future.

"We don't get that much snow in Pittsburgh."

"And we don't get that many earthquakes in San Diego. Everything's a trade-off, I guess."

"Trade-offs. Yeah, I know about them." The words sounded glib, as if they were part of their conversational tennis game, but she sensed there was more to Conner knowing about trade-offs. She waited, thinking he'd explain, but he just sipped his coffee.

Finally, the silence dragged on a beat too long, so she asked, "You don't ever dream of getting out of Pennsylvania and seeing the world?"

"Once upon a time." There was a hint of wistfulness in his voice. "But then I grew up, faced my responsibilities, and here I am."

Yes, there was definitely a story here. She could sense it. But Conner's expression all but screamed off-limits. So she changed the subject. "So, tell me about Saturday's wedding…."

He did just that. Another big society-type gala. The wedding was at the cathedral and the reception at

Lapari. "Just wear something simple. Black slacks, a white shirt. Something that doesn't say 'guest,' but does say 'professional.'"

"Got it, boss." She saluted him.

He laughed. Morgan had a feeling it wasn't something Conner did often. He had more of a brooding, film noir feel to him.

She glanced at her watch. Time to go get ready for her next meeting. "I'm sorry, but I do have to run."

"Meeting that other man." He shook his head in mock dismay.

"For someone who's between jobs, my schedule has been very full of late." She glanced at the check and put down the money and an ample tip. He looked as if he was going to protest, so before he could, she said, "Remember, I invited you, so this one was on me. Thanks, Conner. I look forward to—" she wanted to say getting to know you better, but settled for "—working with you."

"Me, too."

Conner watched as Morgan Miller, his new impromptu assistant, walked out of the coffeehouse.

There was something about her story that didn't quite click, though he wasn't sure what it could be. Her explanation made sense—helping her mother weigh all the options for the business.

To sell, to expand, or just to remain status quo.

But still…

His cell phone rang. He looked at the caller ID. "Hey, Ian. What's up?"

"I'm heading home. He gave me great news."

The *he* in question was his brother's doctor. When

Ian didn't share just what the great news was, Conner asked, "Well?"

"Hurry home after your meeting and I'll fill you in."

Conner couldn't remember the last time he'd heard Ian sound so pleased. "The news is that good?"

He laughed. "Even better."

Conner remembered the moment two years ago when he'd gotten the call about Ian's accident. He'd been packing his bag for his first overseas job, filled with excitement and a sense that he'd made it.

But that one call had changed everything. Worse than letting a dream job go, he'd had to let go of his carefree, slightly irresponsible brother. Ian had become serious, focused.

He'd grown up.

Maybe they both had.

And somewhere along the line, they'd both lost that sense of excitement about life, about its possibilities, and they'd accepted what *was,* putting aside what *could be.*

But Ian's tone said he'd recaptured some enthusiasm with today's news.

"I'll be there soon," Conner promised. "If it's that good, maybe we should plan on celebrating. It's been forever since we went to McGarrity's."

"That would be great. But don't rush your meeting on my behalf. The news will keep."

"The meeting's done. She had another appointment."

"So, was she as hot as you remembered?" Ian asked.

Conner didn't have to think about his answer. "Even hotter."

"Good. It's about time you dated."

"This was business, not a date."

"Who says it can't be both?"

"I don't want another relationship. I want…" Conner wanted his carefree life back, but saying that to his brother would sound cruel. It would seem as if he was complaining, and that was the last thing he'd ever do. He'd made decisions that needed to be made, decisions he'd make again in a heartbeat. He didn't regret them, but that didn't mean he didn't sometimes wish that things were different.

"I want to play the field," he finished.

"Well, there's nothing saying you can't start by playing with her."

Morgan Miller didn't strike him as a player. She'd been all-business in her casual jacket and well-pressed jeans that screamed trying-to-look-casual, even though she didn't quite pull it off. No, she was Professional with a capital *P,* in a totally hot sort of way.

She had these weird streaks in her brown hair. They weren't blond, weren't exactly red, either. He'd lost the thread of the conversation more than once as he tried to figure out just what color they were. Reddish-blond was a lame description, but it was as close as he could come.

"I'll think about it," Conner promised. "I'll be home soon."

He clicked his cell phone shut and wondered about Ms. Miller.

It had been a long time since he'd pursued a woman. His life had revolved around work and Ian's needs. There just hadn't been time for much else.

But Ian didn't need him as much now.

Maybe Conner had time to play the field.

No, not the field.

Morgan Miller.

Yes, maybe he should seriously consider mixing business with pleasure.

CHAPTER SIX

E.J., You know me—I want a plan. I want to know what comes next. But what, if despite all my planning, I get it wrong?

SOMETIMES, BUSINESS COULD be pleasure, Morgan thought as she spotted one man alone at the coffeehouse.

"Mr. Jameson?" Morgan asked, though she was pretty sure the khaki-clad, polo-shirted man was the one her mother had sent her to meet.

"Yes?" He looked puzzled.

"Hi. I'm Morgan Miller. My mother asked me to take this meeting with you."

He gave her an appraising look, then a slow smile spread over his face. "That was very considerate of her."

He stood and pulled out her chair, then gently tucked it under the table after she sat down.

Morgan wasn't used to such courtly manners. Pulling out a chair or opening a door would never have occurred to Marvin. Truth be told, it would never have occurred to her to expect it, though she did like it.

"So, Miss Miller—" he began, his voice silky and low.

She interrupted. "Please, call me Morgan."

"Morgan, then. I'm Mark." He waved down the waitress. "What would you like to drink?"

"Just a diet cola, thanks," she told the woman. "Now, Mr. Jameson." At his raised eyebrow, she corrected herself. "Mark. My mother said you're interested in purchasing Oakland Chair and Dish Rental?"

"Before we start, do you mind if I asked why your mother sent you?" He paused half a beat, then added with a smile, "Not that I mind."

Was he flirting with her?

There was a sort of teasing tone to his not-that-I-mind comment, and a suggestive look in his eyes. Not offensive, but inviting.

It had been years since she'd been flirted with.

Having Marvin off and on again meant that the men in her circle never quite knew if she was on the market or not. Either that, or they simply weren't interested in flirting with her.

Even earlier with Conner, she'd felt a spark, but she wasn't sure she would call any part of their conversation flirting.

So though it had been a long stretch since she'd been involved in a flirtation, she was pretty sure she still recognized the signs—in which case Mark Jameson was indeed flirting with her.

She struggled to remember what his question was.

Ah, why her mother had sent her.

"Mom has worked at the store for years, but being an owner is a whole different ball of wax. Managing things isn't her cup of tea, but it's mine, so she asked me to hear you out."

"Where do you work?" He smiled encouragingly, his eyes locked with hers, giving her his total attention.

"I did work in midlevel management at LM Co. in San Diego, until they downsized my department. Downsized me, more specifically." Maybe she shouldn't have said that. She could have phrased it so it didn't sound as if she'd been canned. "I'm back in Pittsburgh while I weigh my job options."

There. That sounded better. Weighing options was definitely nicer sounding than desperately looking for a new job.

"Are you looking for something locally? Jameson, Inc. is always looking for up-and-coming business-men...and women."

There was a certain something in his voice as he tacked on that "women." Something that said he'd not only noticed she was a woman, but liked that she was.

And despite the fact he wasn't giving her any Connerlike shivers, she enjoyed that he was definitely flirting.

"To be honest, I haven't given any thought to staying in Pittsburgh. I may have grown up here, but over the last few years San Diego has become my home. I'm anxious to get back."

"If you change your mind, let me know. We'll talk."

"I will." Okay, time to get this conversation on the proper track. "But right now, I'd like to talk about

Oakland Chair and Dish Rental and why you're interested in purchasing it."

"We're looking to acquire some good, stable businesses in the greater Pittsburgh area. I've done some checking, and of course would need a more thorough examination of the books, but on the surface, it appears that the store would meet our criteria and give Jameson, Inc. a solid platform to start with, and substantial room for growth."

"Growth. That's the other option I'm exploring for my mother. I do think that any offer we discuss would have to take into account the untapped potential that OCDR has for growth. I know I've been out of town for a long time, but the store's untapped market is a no-brainer."

Mark slid her a file. "That's my initial offer, based on fair market for the two buildings and an estimate of your mother's stock on hand."

Morgan took a sip of cola, opened the file and found his bottom line...then promptly snorted her cola through her nose. It was far more generous than she'd anticipated. "Just an estimate?"

"A low one, I think. Like I said, I'd need a full inventory and client list to be sure, but Neil, our chief appraiser, tends to be rather thorough, and even his estimates are generally on the mark."

"Well." Morgan didn't know what to say. The figure that was still swimming in front of her eyes was more than she'd imagined.

With that kind of money, her mom would be comfortable.

More than comfortable.

"My mother asked for my assistance recently, so I'm afraid you're ahead of me on facts and figures. I need to make some calls, check out what real estate in Oakland is going for, and check out the inventory...."

"Take your time, Morgan. You take a look at what's what, and I think you'll find my offer is more than fair."

"That would be good."

"And rather than meeting at my office, or at your mother's, maybe we could meet for dinner? Faline's, maybe?"

"Faline's?" She was tempted to let out a low, appreciative whistle, but decided it would be less than professional. Still, Faline's was one of the nicest places in town to eat. Park at Station Square, ride up the incline to Mt. Washington. The view at the top was phenomenal, and Faline's food supposedly to die for—if the prices didn't kill you. "I lived in Pittsburgh for years and have never been there."

"Great." He smiled a definite Pierce Brosnan as James Bond sort of smile. "How does Saturday look for you?"

She thought about the wedding and Conner, and shook her head. "Sorry. I already have plans."

"Ah, competition. I enjoy competition. Next Monday then?"

"Monday. That would be fine."

"Then it's a date." He gently placed a hand on hers and flashed her an endearing grin.

A date.

As in a business dinner date?

Or a date date?

Morgan just nodded and said, "Yes, that would be wonderful."

"Do you mind making it early? I have to work the next day. Maybe at six?"

"Early's fine. Six is good," Morgan assured him. "So, Monday then."

His hand was still on hers. She waited expectantly for that rush of adrenaline, of awareness. Waited for her pulse to race and her hands to sweat.

Nothing.

Nada.

Zilch.

That was so odd.

She felt slightly confused as she stood and said, "Thank you, Mr. Jameson. I will look into your proposal and we can discuss the business in depth on Monday."

"It's Mark, remember? And although I'm hoping to discuss the business, I'm hoping we'll have time for some small talk as well."

"Small talk?" she parroted.

"Unrelated to business," he clarified. "Movies, sports, politics. That sort of thing."

"Right. I'll see you next week." She turned and started to hurry out, but he called her name and she turned back. "Yes?"

"You're forgetting my proposal." He picked up the file and handed it to her.

She reached for it and their hands brushed and she felt a slight zap of awareness. It wasn't quite the shock of instant attraction she'd felt with Conner—her pulse wasn't racing and she was pretty sure there wasn't a drop of perspiration anywhere on her body—but there was at least a little something there.

Yes, B. Mark Jameson was definitely more her type than Conner was, even if her reaction to him wasn't as strong.

"And could I ask you a favor?" Mark asked.

"Yes?"

"When you bring along the Chair and Dish Rental information could you also bring a résumé?"

"Why?"

"Like I said, Jameson, Inc. is always looking for talent."

"After this brief meeting, there's no way you could know if I have talent or not. Maybe they downsized my position or maybe I was just covering the fact that they fired me."

As soon as the words were out of her mouth, she wished she could suck them back in.

Here was a man interested in hiring her. Even if she planned on going back to California, there was nothing saying she couldn't at least explore other opportunities.

He laughed and shook his head. "No, Morgan Miller, you weren't fired."

"You're right, I wasn't." She didn't ask why he was so certain. She continued, "And yes, I'll bring you a résumé, though I'll warn you, I meant what I said, I'm really not looking to stay in Pittsburgh."

"Who knows? Maybe I can make it worth your while." He shot her another smile. "It's been a pleasure. Truly, a pleasure."

"Uh. Thanks." Clasping the file, she hurried from the restaurant.

A business date.

He was interested. She might be a rather recent reentry into the dating pool, but she knew he was interested in her.

And he was perfect for her. The perfect combination of suave good looks and business acumen.

Perfect.

And there had been the tiniest spark when they'd touched.

Very tiny.

Almost minuscule.

But still, it could be built on.

And building a small lustfest with a man like Mark wasn't such a bad idea…not a bad idea at all.

CHAPTER SEVEN

E.J., I'm overflowing with men. I've met one who isn't my type, but really does things for me. Things you and I decided long ago not to discuss in depth because you tended to go all big brother on me, wanting to defend my honor. Then I met another who is decidedly my type, and although he stirred only a little interest, I think I can make something of it. Finally, I got home and had a phone call from Marvin. He misses me. When he said that, it made me realize I didn't miss him. Not at all. I guess that's telling. I didn't say that to him—I don't like to be unkind. But I was firm about our absolute zero chances of getting back together. E.J., how did I let things go on that long with him? It makes me question other decisions I've made in the past. E-mail as soon as you get home, or better yet, call. I miss your big brother advice, even if it does sometimes make me crazy.

"Okay, boss, just tell me where to start." Morgan tried to sound chipper and self-assured, though she had a nervous buzz in her belly that she just couldn't seem to shake.

She was wearing a pair of black pants and a white blouse, as per instructions. She'd been ready at two. Neither clothes nor promptness were the source of her anxiety.

To be honest, she'd been on pins and needles all morning and wasn't able to determine exactly why.

It wasn't as if her job with Conner was going to be taxing. As a matter of fact, it would be a piece of cake. She'd do whatever he asked as she supposedly checked out the reception and tried to find new inroads for OCDR.

Actually, she wasn't pretending. This might have started out as a ruse, but she'd like to present her mother with some ideas for the store. And if Annabelle did decide to sell, knowing what new avenues there were in terms of expansion could only solidify her bargaining position with Mark.

So, despite her initial fib, Morgan was here on a legitimate mission.

So why was she sweating?

Not glowing.

Not perspiring.

Sweating. She just hoped her deodorant worked, because the antiperspirant part wasn't doing a thing for her.

"Here, carry this in," Conner said, handing her a case.

"Sure thing."

They entered the beautiful, ornate cathedral. Morgan felt a sense of awe as she glanced into the sanctuary and took in the intricacy of the interior.

Beautifully carved wooden pews, paintings and relics surrounded her. It almost felt like sacrilege to breathe, because it would disrupt the peace.

As if on cue, the peace was shattered by an ear-splitting howl.

A door burst open and a wild-eyed woman wearing a rather obnoxious pink ruffled dress appeared.

"Photographer, right?" she asked brusquely, a note of hysteria in her voice.

Conner nodded, and Morgan just tried to be invisible.

She didn't manage it well enough because the woman looked her up and down appraisingly, then barked, "And you are?"

"My assistant," Conner said smoothly, trying to draw the woman's attention back to him.

It didn't work. She continued to assess Morgan. "What size do you wear?"

"Pardon?"

"Size, girl," she repeated loudly and succinctly, as if Morgan was rather slow-witted and possibly hard of hearing. "What size dress do you wear?"

Morgan looked at Conner, and he simply shrugged, so she told the crazy woman her dress size.

The matron heaved a heavy sigh of relief. "You'll do."

"Do what?" Morgan's earlier nervous buzz was now a roar.

"One of the bridesmaids just called and she's having

car problems. She'll be here in time for the reception, but won't make the wedding ceremony. That's where you come in."

"You want me to go pick her up?" She could take Conner's car and—

"No, of course not. If it was that simple, I'd send my husband. It would be the first bit of use he's been the entire wedding. But picking her up would take too long. It would make the wedding start late. And we have important people on the guest list. The mayor, deans of three of the city's universities. We'll start on time with the proper number of bridesmaids. You'll fill in until Kimberly gets here."

"Ma'am?" Morgan might not be hard of hearing, but she feared she was indeed a bit slow-witted. "I'll do what?"

"You'll be a bridesmaid. No one will even notice. All eyes will be on my daughter, the bride, of course. We just need a body. A body that will fit into Kim's dress. You'll do."

"But—"

"The *mayor* will be here," the woman repeated. "I've spent a year of my life planning this wedding, a small fortune paying for it. Guests will be arriving at any moment and there will be the proper number of bridesmaids marching down that aisle on time or else." Not waiting for any further arguments, the mother of the bride said, "Now, follow me."

"Conner?" Morgan yelped, as if pleading for help.

"Why not?" he said.

Why not? Morgan could think of a host of reasons,

but before she could voice even one, the woman was pushing her toward the door.

"We'll pay a substantial bonus," she called out to Conner, as if that settled it.

"What's your name?" she asked Morgan, not releasing her tight grip.

Morgan wasn't sure the woman even heard her answer as she gave a final push and closed the door behind them.

Like some four-star general, she entered the small changing room and started shouting out commands.

A gaggle of strange women, all dressed in pink, approached. They swarmed toward Morgan like a horde of locusts. There was something in the hands of the lone girl at the back of the pack.

Something large.

Something that looked suspiciously pink and as ruffly as the mother of the bride's gown.

"Here's the dress, Mom," the woman said, thrusting the fussy garment at the general.

"Let's see how this will look," the woman crooned. "Then we'll do your hair and makeup and…"

Morgan didn't have time to think or even cry out before they had her practically naked, then stuffed into the pink monstrosity. Zipping her in required that she hold her breath and suck in all her organs, redistributing them to positions they'd never occupied before. She was pretty sure her breasts increased in size due to the fact that they were almost touching her chin.

"I can't breathe," she said in a strangled voice, hoping for some sympathy.

The women all stared at her a moment, studying her, then looked to the general for her decree.

"She'll do."

Morgan had passed the test. The first test she'd ever hoped she'd fail.

"Now, the hair," the woman cried.

"IT WASN'T THAT BAD," CONNER said soothingly. They were driving from the wedding to the reception. Morgan still looked more than a bit pale.

"Wasn't that bad?" she repeated, punctuating the sentence with a shrill tone he surely couldn't miss. "Maybe not that bad for *you. I* didn't get to breathe deeply for over an hour. You try holding your breath that long. And it might have been worth it if I'd been wearing some fabulous couture sort of dress, not that eighties-flashback horror they stuffed me into."

Her hair still bore traces of whatever goop they'd used. It had lost the polished look that Morgan had each time he'd seen her.

"Come on," he said cajolingly. "You helped them out. They're grateful. And you got a real behind-the-scenes look at a wedding. I bet you have all sorts of ideas for the store. Right?"

Morgan was still shooting daggers at him with her eyes, as if it was his fault she'd been trapped into playing fill-in bridesmaid.

"Yes. I've got a great new idea."

"See, told you."

"Valium. Lithium. The store needs to carry a line of tranquilizers and happy pills for the mother of the bride. The general was overwrought. And the bride? Well, let's not start on her. She was a shrieking, wailing mess."

"They all are before the ceremony. You just wait and see her tonight at the reception. Her groom showed up, they said their I-do's and her bridesmaid finally arrived. The bride's outlook is going to be a lot sunnier than at the ceremony."

"I swear, I never got out of my clothes as quickly as I did when the absent bridesmaid walked in. I feel so...well, able to breathe, now that I'm free of all that frippery."

"Frippery?" He chuckled, but at her glare, saw that he'd made a tactical error.

Despite her grousing in the car, he'd been impressed by what a trouper she'd been, pitching in that way. And he wasn't about to share with her the fact that she'd looked cute in the hideous pink bridesmaid's dress. He'd taken an inordinate number of pictures of her, some he knew he'd never give to the bride; they were for his own personal collection.

Something about Morgan fascinated him. Drew him. He wasn't sure just what. Even now, ranting and carping about the wedding, she was adorable.

Oh, he doubted that's how she'd want to be described, but there it was. She was cute. And it was all he could do not to lean over and kiss her.

Thankfully, they pulled up at the reception hall before his inclination won out over his good sense.

"We're here," he announced.

If the reception was anything like the wedding, it was going to be an interesting evening.

MORGAN STUDIED THE BEAUTIFUL country club with its perfectly manicured lawns, huge old trees and magnificent stone entryway. She breathed deep, thankful to be out of the close confines of the car. Being so near to Conner made her heart race and her entire body perspire.

She was glad to be back in her own clothes, and not the unfortunate bridesmaid's dress, for the ride. She'd have hated to hand the girl back a sodden gown. After all, it was ugly enough without being drippy.

She stood outside the car, wishing she dared flap her arms and dry them a bit.

"This is it?" she asked, stalling for time. After all, if they'd stopped in front of the building, it must be the place.

"Nice, eh?" he said.

"More than nice."

They got out and unloaded his equipment. As he handed her a camera bag, he came close enough that she couldn't help but notice again how good he smelled.

Very good.

She followed him into the building, playing the dutiful girl Friday, but actually she was pondering Conner.

She wasn't sure what scent he wore, but she'd like to get a bottle and just spray her pillow with it. She was pretty sure it would lead to some amazing dreams.

She'd never known she was such a scent junkie, but it appeared that she was.

"Okay, now in that cardboard box you'll find disposable cameras," explained Conner. "Take them around to the tables, and make sure that whoever's sitting there knows we hope they'll use them up before the night's over."

"Great."

Carrying the box of cameras, Morgan began to distribute them. It was a relief to get a bit of distance between herself and Conner. A bigger relief when she realized she'd put some distance between herself and her thoughts as well.

She was pretty sure her armpits were drying, and her heart rate had definitely settled into a more normal rhythm…well, right up to the minute she spotted the two women bearing down on her.

"Morgan!"

"Nikki? Tessa? What are you two doing here?" Morgan's heart rate was once again racing, but not in the same he's-hot-and-smells-good sort of way. And not in a filling-in-for-a-missing-bridesmaid sort of way. Rather in an oh-shit kind of way—what would Conner think of her if he found out? "You're friends of the bride and groom?"

That was it. She tried to calm herself down. Yes, that had to be it. Nikki and Tessa knew the happy couple and were invited guests. But when Nikki laughed, Morgan knew her friend hadn't been invited, and her hopes faded away.

"No. Not at all. Tessa and I took your advice."

Oh, no. It couldn't be. But even as she asked, "What advice?" she knew very well what it could be and, with her luck, probably was.

"Why—" Nikki dropped her voice "—crashing, of course. Sunny refused to come, but Annabelle helped me and Tess find a reception to crash. And here we are."

"Yippee." Tessa had never been able to, or more accurately, never felt inclined to mask her feelings. If she was unhappy, everyone knew it. And Tessa was definitely not happy about being here.

Well, that made two of them. Morgan was definitely less than enthusiastic. What if the General found out? Morgan couldn't imagine the mother of the bride would have much of a sense of humor about party crashers.

"We didn't know you'd be here," Nikki said. "But I'm so glad you are. It makes it even more fun."

"I can't believe you went along with her crazy plan," Morgan said to Tessa.

"I almost didn't. But Nikki was bound and determined to get a column out of this, and as her attorney I'm bound and determined to keep her out of jail. Between you and me, I don't think it's just a column. She—" Tessa pointed at the obviously excited Nikki "—is hoping to meet the man of her dreams here. You know, the same one she hopes she'll meet on every bad blind date, and at every bar she visits. She can't seem to shake the fairytale belief in true love."

"Hey," Nikki protested, "don't think I can't tell you're sneering at me or the idea of true love, Tessa Jean Caldwell. You don't have a romantic bone in your body. It could happen. The man I'm destined to be with could be here, right now. That's how it happened for Annabelle all those years ago with Morgan's dad. And you—" she turned to Morgan, obviously looking for support "—met the hot photographer while you were crashing."

"Shh," Morgan hissed.

Nikki dropped her voice a bit. "By the way, where is he? We want to check him out."

Oh, yeah, Morgan could just picture that.

Nikki would walk over, introduce herself and ask if he had any friends so that they could all double. Blind dates were once Nikki's favorite part-time occupation, and from what Morgan had heard, that hadn't changed a bit during the time she'd been gone.

Morgan shook her head. "Oh, no you don't. You totally stay out of his way. I don't want any pictures of the two of you turning up when he develops his film."

Just then the man in question, camera in hand, approached them, poised to take a picture.

Thinking quickly, Morgan moved between the camera and her two party crashing friends, just as it flashed.

"Uh, sorry," she told him.

And though she wasn't exactly sorry she'd blocked Conner's shot, she was truly sorry for a lot of other things.

Sorry that the Fates were against her.

Sorry her mother had aided and abetted her two friends in their crashing exploits.

Sorry that Morgan found herself in such an absurd situation.

Sorry she'd left a decidedly normal life in San Diego and found herself traveling down a rabbit hole into Pittsburgh, Pennsylvania.

"Morgan, you ruined my shot," Conner complained. No, not complained. That sounded as if he was whining, and he definitely wasn't whining. Instead, he was scowling.

Note to self: never get between a photographer and his subject.

"Sorry," she said again. "I'll be more careful."

Conner moved a step beyond Morgan and shot her friends a killer smile. "Ladies, would you mind my trying again?"

Even as Nikki said, "No, feel free," and started to pose, Morgan blocked his shot again.

"Sorry, but the bride was hoping you'd get a picture of the cake before her niece gets her fingers into it again. They already had to reposition it to hide the missing rose."

Conner gave her an odd look, then nodded. "All right. Did you finish passing out the cameras?"

"I was just giving some to these two ladies before coming to find you for the bride." Morgan dropped her voice. "They needed more instructions than most. I don't think the brunette's very sharp." She paused, then added, "The bride seemed very anxious about the cake."

"I'd better run. I'll get a picture of you two ladies later."

"We'd love it," Nikki called merrily.

Conner gave a small wave, then hurried across the reception hall.

"No. You wouldn't love it," Morgan corrected her friend.

"I wouldn't?"

"You wouldn't. I warn you, Nikki, if I look through these pictures and find you in any of them, I'm going to get a particular old photo of mine out and mail a copy to your mom. I'm pretty sure you can guess which one I'm talking about."

"You wouldn't." Nikki was obviously trying to sound assured, but wasn't able to hide the hint of doubt that crept into her tone. "Would you?"

"Try me."

Nikki's mom was as by-the-book as Morgan's mom was doesn't-even-own-a-book.

"She'd have a hissy fit if she saw her only daughter shooting a moon," Morgan assured her. "And after you denied so vehemently toilet-papering the principal's yard, the photo would say otherwise."

"I can't believe you'd threaten me like this."

Morgan knew Nikki wanted her to feel guilty, but all she felt was relief that maybe she'd found a way to control her rather wild and spontaneous friend. "I can't believe you crashed my wedding."

"It's not your wedding, and we didn't know you'd be here."

"Girls," Tessa scolded. "No fighting. I'm here to see to it no one ends up in jail, and a brawl might wreck that goal."

"You heard her—she threatened to tell my mother," Nikki said. "She's been on the West Coast far too long. It's sucked away her sense of adventure."

"I have a sense of adventure. A great sense of adventure," Morgan protested. "If I didn't, I wouldn't be here in this absurd situation. You're just trying to blow my cover."

"Oh, I didn't realize that you had a monopoly on crashing."

Morgan realized Nikki was right; she was here under false pretenses, just like they were. "Oh, go, have fun, just don't let Conner take any pictures of you. Please, don't wreck this for me."

The "please" must have softened Nikki's ire, because she said, "He is awfully cute."

"Cute?" Tessa scoffed. "Hot. He's downright burn-your-briefs hot."

"Was that a joke, Tessa Jean?" Nikki asked, laughing.

"Just because I'm an attorney doesn't mean I don't have a sense of humor. Lawyers are funny."

Nikki snorted.

Tessa glared at her, then turned back to Morgan. "I won't let her wreck it for you. She'll behave, I promise."

"Good. Thanks. I'd better finish delivering these cameras." Morgan plopped one in each of her friends' hands. "Take some pictures, just don't have any taken of you."

Nikki looked at the disposable camera and nodded. "Oh, and before you go, we wanted to be sure you're coming to brunch tomorrow."

"Will *she* be there?"

"Would we have asked you if she were coming?" Tessa replied.

Morgan knew they wouldn't. "Then, yes, I'd love to. I didn't realize how much I've missed Sunday brunches… missed all of you."

"Well, I doubt you'll miss us tonight, so we won't stay long," Tessa assured her. "Once Nikki's had her adventure and discovered her true love isn't lurking in the shadows, we're going. If we don't say goodbye, don't worry. We'll see you in the morning."

"And I'll tell you all about my lucky night, because despite what doubting Tessa thinks, there could be a Mr. Right for me right here." Nikki started scanning the crowd, as if she expected to find him immediately.

If Morgan had any luck at all, Nikki wouldn't spot anyone, and she and Tessa would both leave before Conner caught up with them again.

And imagine Nikki calling Conner cute! She snorted. Was she blind?

Tessa was right—he was much more than cute. He was gorgeous. And if he found out about all this crashing, she might lose whatever chance she had to experience that heat up close and personal.

Morgan hurried away, very much aware of how she'd almost had her cover blown. Her heart rate was racing again, and she was sweating even more.

Profusely.

And this time it had nothing to do with Conner's good looks, and everything to do with almost getting found out.

This would teach her to take a walk on the wild side. As soon as she finished this brief little foray, she was heading back to safety. No more fantasies about nice-smelling men.

She found him by the cake.

"Did you get the picture before more roses were eaten?"

"The little scamp got another one, but I managed to find an untouched side to photograph, and simply twisted the cake topper for the shot, so we're fine." He gave Morgan a long, hard look. "Speaking of fine, are you? Fine, that is?"

"Yes. Of course." She paused and added, "Why?"

"You seemed a bit…well, not quite fine a few minutes ago."

"Sorry." She tried to think of an excuse. "Ah, one of the men was flirting with me, and I wasn't quite sure how to get out of it without offending him."

Another lie.

She was really racking them up.

Conner's expression darkened. "Want me to talk to him?" His voice was lower than normal and there was a hint of danger in it.

Morgan felt warmed and flushed at the sound. "No. I told him I was involved with someone else, but appreciated his interest. I let him down easy."

"Oh," Conner said. "You have a boyfriend?"

Could that be disappointment in his expression? Morgan hoped so.

"No," she assured him. "It was a fib." Now she was lying about lying? "I didn't want to tell him he wasn't my type."

"Just who is your type?" Conner asked, as he took a roll of film from his pocket.

Just a week or so ago, Morgan could have answered him without a moment's hesitation. But now? Maybe her taste was changing, or maybe there was something about Conner that made her want to break from her type. But either way, she didn't have anything definitive to say, so simply shrugged. "My type changes at whim."

"So you just made someone up?"

"Well, sort of. I mean, it's not like I'm dating this fictional boyfriend, but the man does in fact exist. You see, I told him I was dating the photographer."

"Oh." Conner's lips curved slowly, his smile spreading like butter on warm toast. "And this photographer? Is he good-looking?"

"Not wanting you to get an inflated ego, I'll just answer that I'm sure some women think so."

"How about you?" he asked.

"Well, I'm dating him, aren't I?" she teased.

"That doesn't really answer my question, does it?"

"I'd love to continue our verbal Ping-Pong match, but don't you have a reception to photograph?"

"Yes. But this reception won't last forever. I'll ask you again."

"You can always ask."

He laughed. "But you won't always answer? Is that what you're saying?"

"I like being a woman of mystery." She was flirting. And she was enjoying the experience.

CHAPTER EIGHT

E.J., if you'd asked me a few months ago I'd have assured you that I didn't know how to play those man-woman games you're so good at. But I find myself blatantly flirting with Conner, and as surprising as that seems, it's even more surprising how much fun it is....

MORGAN WAS STILL ENJOYING flirting with Conner as the reception wound down.

It was out of character for her.

Way out of character.

She'd dated Thomas for years, then left and sort of fell into a relationship with Marvin. Neither had required much in the way of effort on her part.

If something developed with Conner it would be because she actively pursued it.

She felt…maybe *empowered* was the right word?

And maybe a bit victorious. Nikki and Tessa had left with no one the wiser. Now that they were gone without having revealed her plot, Morgan couldn't wait until breakfast to hear all the details.

She wasn't sure where Gina had been last Sunday, or would be this Sunday, but hadn't asked because mainly she didn't care.

She was way beyond her old friend's betrayal, and simply didn't want to spend time with her.

"Hey, you did great," Conner said, coming up behind her and setting his camera on the table. "We're done for the night. I sure appreciated the help."

"I gathered up all the disposable cameras." She nodded at the box she'd put them into.

"Great. I'll hold on to them." He started gathering his equipment. "Ready?"

"Yes. I don't know that I ever realized how grueling taking pictures at a wedding could be. I'm beat."

"Too tired to grab a bite?"

She was about to say that she'd love to get something to eat when she remembered Gilligan. "I have a dog, and though my mom promised to let him out this afternoon, I bet his bladder is probably bursting."

"Oh." Conner looked disappointed.

"But…"

He jumped on the word. "But?"

"But we could grab something and eat it at my place, if you don't mind."

He was grinning. "Sure, that sounds great."

Morgan paused a moment. Though she might lust after Conner a bit—more than a bit—taking a man home on a first date wasn't her thing. Not that this was a date, but still, there had been that brief flirtation. He could have unrealistic, and not-gonna-happen at-least-not-to-night ideas about the evening.

"Uh, I don't want you to think I'm inviting you to my place to…well, to do more than have dinner. I mean—"

"You're not that kind of girl." It was a statement, firm and filled with certainty.

"Yes. I mean no." Morgan was pretty sure she was sweating again. There were times like this that she wished she were that kind of girl. "I mean, yes, you're correct, I'm not like that."

"I already knew that, Morgan." His voice was a whispered caress. "If I thought you were, I wouldn't *want* to have dinner with you. I guess you could say I'm not that kind of a guy."

"Then, dinner—just dinner—it is."

If she was that kind of girl he wouldn't be interested. He'd just admitted as much. What would he think if he knew she had, in fact, blatantly chased him?

It didn't matter, because he'd never know.

They gathered up the rest of Conner's equipment, stopped at a store and bought two subs and a bottle of wine, then headed to Morgan's.

"I'd have invited you to my place," Conner said, "but my brother lives with me."

"That wouldn't have bothered me. I'd love to meet him."

"Maybe next time, then?"

Next time. There was going to be a next time.

Morgan felt warm all over.

"I'd like that…. This is it," she said.

He pulled into the drive. "Nice. You have classy taste."

"The taste was my uncle Auggie's. I inherited the place earlier this year."

"Still, I like it. It looks homey."

Morgan realized that it was indeed homey. Maybe that was why, despite her best intentions, she hadn't changed a thing.

She opened the door, flipping on the lights as Gilligan bounded toward her. Well, waddled was more like it. He seemed happy to see her.

And when the dog spotted her guest, he immediately began sniffing Conner's leg, his doggie hips wiggling.

"I think he likes me," Conner said, leaning down to pat his head. "What's his name?"

"Gilligan. My uncle had a thing for the show," she answered before he asked. "The dog's ancient. Fourteen. That's like ninety-eight in doggie years. Back in his heyday, he was a humper. But now arthritis has set in and he just wishes he could. See his hips moving?"

"Uh…"

Stupid. Stupid. Stupid. She was babbling about her geriatric, wannabe-humping dog because the realization that she had Conner at her house was sinking in.

"I'd better let him out," she said, anxious for a bit of respite. "The kitchen's this way."

She led Conner and Gilligan down the hall, then flipped on the overhead light and thanked the kitchen gods that she wasn't a cook. The room was pristine.

"Make yourself at home," she said as she unlocked and opened the back door. "Come on, Gilligan."

Conner set their subs on the counter. "Where are the glasses?"

"They're in the righthand cupboard over the sink."

She was just shutting the back door when a shadow moved into her line of sight.

"Hi, honey," her mom said cheerily.

Morgan gave a little squeal. "Mom? What are you doing skulking in the backyard at this time of night?"

"I don't skulk, Morgan Elisabeth. I saw a car pull in and thought I'd come see what you were up to tonight." She walked into the kitchen. "Why, hello." There was appreciation in her voice.

Appreciation Morgan shared, although at the moment her annoyance with her mother overrode it.

"Hi," Conner said.

"I'm Morgan's mom, Annabelle Miller." She laughed and quickly launched into the spiel she used whenever meeting someone new. "And yes, I know I don't look anywhere near old enough to be her mother. I was practically a baby myself when I had her. And you are?"

"I'm Morgan's…friend. Conner. Conner Danning. We were just having an impromptu dinner."

"Don't let me interrupt." Annabelle turned back to Morgan and winked in obvious approval of finding a man in her kitchen. "Honey, I just stopped by because Nikki called. She's worried she's in trouble for crashing—"

"Crashing her car. Yes, I know all about it, and she's an adult, so she doesn't need to worry about a lecture from me." Hands on her mother's shoulders, Morgan steered her toward the still-open back door. "You just rest easy, and tell her to do the same. I'll call her myself after my company leaves."

"Her car? But—"

"Really, not to worry, Mom." Morgan eased her outside. "It's all good. But right now, I have a guest, so let's talk later."

"But—"

"'Night."

Annabelle finally took Morgan's not-too-subtle hint and left, passing Gilligan as he came back into the house and flopped on the mat in front of the door.

"Is he okay?" Conner asked, eyeing the old dog.

"Going to the bathroom tires him. Walking tires him, too. Actually, I'm discovering pretty much any type of movement tires him."

"Discovering?"

"I inherited him along with the house…and two cats, supposedly."

"Supposedly? You have supposed cats?"

She laughed. "That's about the size of it. I'm pretty sure they're here in the house somewhere. I mean, Mom brought them over when I arrived, but when she opened the crate, they streaked out in a blur. I haven't seen them since. But their food's gone every day and I've never seen Gilligan eating it, so I'm pretty sure they're around. I just think they miss Uncle Auggie. He really wasn't my uncle, just our lifelong neighbor. After his wife died, Mom and I were all the family he had left. She's worked for him forever."

Morgan was babbling again. That was almost as bad as sweating. Maybe worse. After all, people might miss the fact that you were sweating, but babbling sort of announced itself and was hard to miss.

What on earth was happening with her? She was a grown woman who'd been in relationships before.

Maybe she didn't want this to be a relationship? Just a fling. A short, sweet, sweaty fling.

She opened the bottle of wine, thankful for a distraction.

"Your mother worked for your uncle at the Chair and Dish Rental?"

"Yes." There. That wasn't babbling. She set the wine on the table as Conner passed her a sub.

"And now that she owns it, she's thinking of expanding."

Morgan took her seat. "She's thinking about a number of options." That was true as well. "You see, Mom doesn't have much of a head for business. She's asked me to help while I'm home."

"Home from…?" He took a bite and made an appreciative groaning sound.

Morgan filled him in on all the gory details.

"Working for your mom, helping her find ways to expand the company." He smiled. "Spending time helping me so you can do some market research. That's very nice of you."

Nice wasn't quite the word to describe how she felt.

Slimy.

Underhanded.

Conner saying he believed she wasn't that kind of girl. Ha. If only he knew.

She should just tell him now. Confess the whole thing. Tell him she'd embellished the notion of expanding the store just to get to spend some time with him, because she thought he was hot.

She realized that confessing would show him she was that kind of girl.

"No, I'm not that nice, I promise."

Okay, that girl or not, she was going to do it. She was going to admit that she'd made up the story in order to see him. He might be flattered. "Conner, I wanted to say—"

But it was hard to say much of anything, much less have Conner hear it. A yowl that seemed to originate in the hall drowned out the rest of her sentence and also woke Gilligan, who lumbered to his feet and started barking maniacally.

"The cats?" Conner asked loudly.

"I'd have to say yes. Do you see them?"

"No."

"Here, Thurston and Lovey. Come here, guys."

There was no more yowling, but Gilligan didn't seem inclined to stop barking.

"Maybe the dog is why the cats hide. He doesn't seem overly fond of them."

"Maybe. I don't know. I'd barely pulled into the driveway when my mother came marching across the yard with a cat carrier in one hand and Gilligan's leash in the other."

"So far this has been an interesting first date." Conner chuckled.

Date.

The word hung there between them for a pregnant moment.

"I—" They both started to talk at once, but were interrupted by Conner's cell phone.

He glanced at the display screen. "Sorry. I have to take this." He flipped open the phone and walked out the back door to escape the noise.

"Look what you all did." Morgan scolded Gilligan, because the cats were still hiding. "Nice manners."

Gilligan gave one more loud bark and then, having used up all his energy chasing the phantom cats, plopped onto the linoleum and gazed at her balefully.

"I don't know if your apology is going to work this time."

"But an apology is all I have to offer," Conner said, coming back in. "You were talking to me?"

"No. The dog."

"Well, I hope my apology is greeted with a more favorable result."

"And just what are you apologizing for?"

"I've got to go. But I'd like to pick up this dating thing again another time."

Her brazen ability to flirt seemed to disappear, and Morgan was left feeling suddenly shy. She nodded. "I'd like that."

"Are you up for another wedding next week? I have one on Friday night. I mean, if you have enough information now I understand…." He let the sentence trail off.

"Another wedding would be great." It wasn't the wedding, but just seeing him again would be great, yet she didn't say that out loud.

"Great," he said, echoing her. He took a step toward her. "Thanks for the help today."

"Thanks for letting me."

"If this was a date, there's a ritual for saying goodnight."

"Yes, if that's what this was, we should follow it. I think it's pretty much a jinx if we don't." She wondered if kissing Conner would be everything she thought it would be. She didn't have long to wonder as he drew nearer and their lips finally met.

It was everything a first kiss should be—soft, not demanding, an introduction of possibilities, of what could be. Of what they might have.

"So, I guess it was a date," Conner said, smiling.

Morgan knew she was grinning like crazy, but she couldn't help it. For the first time in a very long time, she felt completely happy. "I guess it was."

"I'll call you next week, if that's okay."

"It's more than okay." She walked him to the front door, Gilligan padding along dutifully after her.

She opened the door, but rather than go through, Conner hesitated.

"Maybe we should say goodbye again. After all, we were together on that long walk from the kitchen," he said, trying to appear the soul of seriousness.

"You do have a point," she said, playing along, since to be honest another good-night seemed like a pretty good idea to her.

This time she took charge, leaning into him, pressing her lips firmly against his. But control didn't last long for either of them. The kiss quickly deepened, intensified…all but burned.

"The perfect second kiss," she murmured.

"Pardon?"

"Well, I thought the kiss in the kitchen was a perfect first one and…"

"This was the perfect second." He reached out and lightly ran a finger down her cheek. "My thought as well. But I really do have to go now."

"We'll talk next week," she said, though there was

an underlying question, even a need to be assured that this interlude wasn't a fluke.

"I don't want to wait until the wedding on Friday to see you. What about dinner? Tuesday night? My place. I'll introduce you to my brother."

"And cook?"

"Maybe. If it doesn't work, which my cooking frequently doesn't, at least we can order takeout."

She felt giddy with success. Her plan had worked. Immediately after, she felt another pang of guilt. She should just confess to Conner that she'd made up the ploy in order to see him again.

After all, she was giving her mother an option to selling. Her work with Conner was useful.

So she forced a hopefully guilt free smile and said, "Yes. I'd like that."

CONNER LEFT MORGAN'S HOUSE AND was driving toward his place when he realized he was humming. He wasn't sure what song it was supposed to be, but he realized it had been a long time since he'd felt happy enough to hum.

Dinner with Morgan on Tuesday.

Yes, his life was coming back together. Slowly but surely. He stopped humming as he wondered what was up with Ian.

Conner frowned, realizing he'd all but forgotten his brother while he was kissing Morgan. Though the moment had only lasted a few brief seconds, he felt guilty.

To be honest, he'd almost forgotten his own name while he was kissing Morgan.

But he wasn't kissing her now, and he wasn't forgetting anything, either.

He wasn't forgetting the call almost two years ago. That one call had changed everything.

"Hello."

"Mr. Danning?" an unfamiliar voice had asked.

He remembered the stab of dread. He didn't believe in premonitions, but he remembered a feeling in his gut that had told him something was terribly wrong, he'd answered, "Yes," and had held his breath.

"This is St. Kathryn's Hospital. Your brother, Ian…"

Today, Conner could still feel the rush of fear, and couldn't remember a minute of the drive to the hospital, or the doctor patiently explaining the injuries his brother sustained when his car was hit head-on by a drunk driver. A few terms like CT, MRI and compression fractures had penetrated, but most of it hadn't.

Conner had eventually cut the doctor off. "I just want to see him."

The man had nodded. "Yes. But I want you to be prepared. It's not as bad as it's going to look."

And it wasn't as bad. It was worse. Ian had been in traction, a mass of bruises and cuts. What followed were months of surgeries and rehabilitation.

But they'd made it through all that.

Ian was now moving into his own place.

And Conner had started putting out feelers, hoping to get back to building the career he'd always dreamed of.

He'd postponed that dream and didn't regret it. But he was ready to pick up his life at the point where he'd left it.

He pulled up in front of their Lawn Street rental, parked and hurried in.

He'd been so pleased when he'd found this place. His old apartment had been on a second floor, and Ian's had a flight of stairs from the street to the front door. Neither had worked for Ian's new circumstances.

This place was surrounded by predominantly college housing, but there was a bedroom and bath on the first floor, and only three stairs to the front door. Given the hilly nature of Pittsburgh, the lack of stairs was what had sold Conner on it. A small ramp was all it took to make it work for Ian.

The light was off in the living room. The house seemed unoccupied. "Ian?"

"In here." His brother's voice came from his bedroom.

Conner hurried back. "So, what's up?" He opened the door and didn't need to ask anything else. "What happened?"

"I just took a small spill. I think I need a few stitches. I'd drive myself over to the E.R., but I figured you'd be back soon, and remembered how you enjoy feeling useful."

Ian grinned, but it was forced and they both knew it. He was pressing a cloth to the gaping slash across his forehead.

Conner knew better than to show any sympathy. Ian would read it as pity. Not much could anger his easygoing brother, but that would.

So Conner forced his own smile and tried to infuse levity into his voice, which he didn't actually feel. "So, what's the other guy look like?"

"The shower. It doesn't look any the worse for wear."

"Well, let's get down to the hospital. I know this is your lame-ass attempt at picking up women."

"Hey, if I'm lucky, the doctor will be hot, single and..."

"Hopefully female?"

Ian grinned. "That's a given."

"Then let's go meet the future Mrs. Ian Danning."

Conner pushed Ian's chair, which only showed that his brother was hurt worse than he was letting on. Ian hadn't used the wheelchair in months, and even then wouldn't have tolerated being pushed.

"Thanks," he said, the humor gone. "You'd finished, hadn't you?"

"Yeah." Conner thought about Morgan at the door. "Yeah, I'd just said my good-nights and was on my way home."

"Great. Sorry. I just didn't realize how tired I was and…"

"Hey, don't worry about it. Let's go see if we can find that gorgeous female doctor."

"If you're lucky, maybe there will be a cute nurse as well."

Conner didn't say anything, but he didn't think it would matter how cute the nurse was, his interests were definitely elsewhere.

Yes, his sights were set on a certain brunette with reddish highlights, a quick smile, an aging ex-humping bulldog, invisible cats and an offbeat mom. Morgan Miller packed a wallop with her kisses.

Conner wasn't interested in a long-term anything, but she was planning to go back to…San Diego, was it? So maybe that didn't matter.

Since she was planning on leaving Pittsburgh as well, she couldn't want long-term, either. But if things went further than a mere kiss, he'd have to be sure.

Tuesday night.

Maybe he'd need to know on Tuesday night.

CHAPTER NINE

ANNABELLE HAD FELT ELATED AFTER leaving Morgan and her photographer date. She knew she wouldn't be able to sleep, so she'd headed to the Oakland Café. It was one of the few bars in town that catered to an older clientele, rather than the college crowd.

She scanned the private room at the back of the bar. She hadn't come here intending to crash anything, but the party was too tempting to not at least have a look.

There'd been a discreet, tasteful sign on the door: Aldous Markam. She wasn't sure what milestone good old Aldous was celebrating, but she'd seen too many well-dressed, salt-and-pepper-haired men—some with obvious dates or wives, but a number who were tantalizingly solo—go into the private room not to check it out.

She followed, walking into the large room as if she owned it. That was part of the trick to crashing she'd tried to share with Morgan: own whatever party you're crashing and no one will question your right to be there.

Not that Morgan paid attention to her mother's sage advice. If she had, she might not have spent the last few years so far away from home, her family and friends.

Annabelle pushed aside worries about her daughter and made her way through the crowd, picking up snippets of conversations.

"…and that time Al got us tossed out of that casino in Vegas…"

"…he said, no, officer, I just like it like that…."

"…women. Never met a man who could sweet-talk a woman out of her lacy underthings as quickly as Al could."

Annabelle decided then and there that Aldous might have been cursed with an unfortunate first name, but he'd overcome it and become a man worth knowing. A man who could talk her out of her lacy underthings and her current lack of a man status.

She scanned the guests, looking for this depantsing Al. The gathering was predominantly people in her age bracket, so she felt confident he was within her dating range.

She tugged at her sage-green dress. She knew it didn't do much for her coloring, but more than made up for that by what it did for her figure. She was ready to take on Al, if she could just find him.

Annabelle spotted a very nice looking man in the back corner, to the right of a buffet table. Tall, obviously not one of those older men who had grown into a couch potato, with dark hair, and only a touch of gray at the temples. Yes, that gray was ample enough to declare he was well within Annabelle's dating range. And the fact that no woman was clinging to his arm, or even flitting about in the vicinity, proclaimed him fair game.

She hoped—really hoped—that this was pants-talking Al.

She gave him the look she'd practiced throughout her teen years and had finally perfected in her twenties. During the intervening decades it had grown rusty. Her husband hadn't required feminine wiles. Come-and-get-me looks had been replaced by much bolder whispered invitations.

But now she was pulling the look back out and hoping it hadn't lost its punch. She added an extra oomph before she said, "Hi," in her lowest, sexiest voice. The man she hoped was Al regarded her with a look she hoped meant interest. "Are you a friend or colleague of Al's?"

Damn. Wrong Man. Still, he was cute. And there had been that look that flitted across his face as he'd said hi.

"I'm Paul," he added.

"Annabelle. A friend..." She didn't want this man to think she was one of *those* kinds of friends to Al, so she added, "A casual friend."

"I'm sorry for your loss, then."

Loss?

She turned and scanned the room. She spotted a small table with flower arrangements and a picture.

A wake.

She had inadvertently crashed a wake.

Never one to let an opportunity pass her by, Annabelle turned back to Paul, her mind made up. "So, Paul, how long had you known Al?"

CHAPTER TEN

E.J., No word about any of my résumés. I hate waiting, hate having my future in limbo. And speaking of limbo, where are you? I called the hospital and they said you're fine, but in some small village for another few weeks. I'm glad you're okay, but an occasional phone call would be nice.

If you'd phone, I know you'd ask what's up. Well, I have a meeting with Mark on Monday. Although since we're meeting over dinner, and not in an office, maybe it's more than just business. Do I want it to be more than just business? He's definitely my type. Then I have a date with Conner the-hunky-photographer-who's-not-my-type on Tuesday.

In the meantime, I'm having breakfast with friends again today. They crashed the wedding I worked last night. I'm torn between wanting to hear how it went, and wanting to yell because they almost blew it for me with Conner…

I'm falling into a routine here. Things are starting to feel comfortable. Normal in a rather abnormal way.

That makes me nervous.

ON SUNDAY MORNING, DESPITE the fact that working for Conner last night had been exhausting, Morgan found her steps were light as she walked into the diner. She was anxious to hear all about Nikki and Tessa's crashing experience. Of course, after she'd heard the details, she planned to warn them off future crashing…at least of any reception Conner was working.

Sunny was the only one at the table.

"Hey, where is everyone?" Morgan asked as she took her chair.

"Nikki called and croaked that she was going to be late. And Tessa's always late, but never calls. So it's you and me for a bit."

That was fine with Morgan. She scooted her chair closer. "So, I got the fun version last week at breakfast, and we've really just surface talked at OCDR. This gives me a chance to ask, really, how are you?"

"Really?" Sunny repeated. "Really, I'm fine. Johnny is healthy and wonderful. He spends most Saturday nights with Mom so I can go out and date…at least that's always her hope. In actuality, I tend to catch up on the housework, enjoy the bit of quiet, then come here Sunday mornings for my friend fix. Work is fun— which, knowing your mother, you understand—and pays the bills. So, to repeat myself, really, I'm fine."

That all sounded well and good, but Morgan worried

that good wasn't enough for Sunny. Her friend deserved more than cleaning her house on Saturday nights, then meeting friends for Sunday brunch. She deserved so much more. Unbridled happiness at the very least.

Sunny deserved someone who would love her as her ex never had.

Maybe she sensed Morgan's thoughts, for she quickly continued, "My life might seem small to you, Tessa and Nikki, but I'm content."

"Maybe," Morgan said softly, taking her friend's hand, "maybe we all want more than contentment for you."

Sunny shrugged. "And maybe once upon a time I had bigger dreams, but then there was Johnny and now all my dreams are for him. I'm—"

She didn't get to finish the sentence because at that moment Nikki practically tiptoed up, wearing dark sunglasses. Without saying a word she took her seat and put her head down on the table with an audible thump.

"Long night?" Morgan said with a laugh.

Nikki just growled in response.

"I don't think she wants to talk about it," Tessa said as she approached the table and took her own seat. "But I don't mind."

"Do tell." Sunny leaned forward with definite interest.

"Well, we crashed the party Morgan was working, and there was this lawyer—" Tessa's sentence stopped dead in its tracks.

Morgan realized she wasn't going to hear about the lawyer today because there was someone sitting in the seat across from her. The seat that had remained empty last week.

The seat Morgan had never wanted to see filled again.

"Excuse me," she said stiffly as she stood. "I'll get the details some other time. I have to go."

"Morgan, please wait," said Gina, as she jumped up from the table. The fiancé-stealing, ex-best-friend. The woman responsible for Morgan's very broken heart.

Although, come to think about it, her heart had long since healed. But still, it had been broken, and Gina was responsible for it needing to heal.

"I have to go," Morgan repeated. She forced herself to walk to the front of the restaurant, when what she really wanted to do was run.

"Morgan," Gina called from behind her.

"We've got nothing to say."

Gina grabbed her elbow and Morgan turned, ready to tell her to keep her fiancé-stealing hands off of her. But the words died in her mouth when she noticed the tears in Gina's eyes. "Please?"

Morgan wanted to say no.

To scream no.

But she couldn't force that small word out. It died in her throat, and no other took its place. With nothing left to do, she simply nodded.

Gina sank into a chair at the nearest table, and Morgan found herself following suit, almost against her will. Still, she couldn't bring herself to speak.

When the silence grew pregnant and Morgan was struggling to think of something, anything, to say to fill the void, Gina said, "I'm sorry."

Morgan had never planned on talking to Gina again, so she hadn't given much thought to how a conversation between them would go. But if she had, she'd have expected excuses, not an apology, and certainly not the tears that were forming in Gina's eyes.

"I loved him. I still love him." Gina's voice was all but a whisper. "But I hurt you and I'm sorry for that. So sorry. I've missed you so much. All the things I wanted you with me for, I realized I didn't have the right to ask. Wanting you there was selfish, but knowing that didn't stop me from wishing you *were* there. I understand your feelings and we all decided that until you leave, we'll split Sundays. I won't come back on one of your mornings, but I needed to say, to tell you, that the thing I regret most in life is that I hurt you. That Thomas and I hurt you."

Morgan didn't know what to say to that, and before she could put together any coherent thought, Gina stood. "That's all I wanted to say. Thanks for listening."

She left.

Morgan sat at the table for several long minutes.

"Morgan." It was Tessa's voice.

Morgan didn't want to see Tessa or Nikki at that moment any more than she had wanted to see Gina.

"I've got to go," she said, hurrying out of the restaurant, starting the long walk home. Her heavy thoughts weighed down each and every step.

For the last five years she'd remembered Thomas and Gina with bitterness. But today, seeing Gina, listening to her apology...

Morgan could still feel the pain, but it wasn't as raw as it had been. As a matter of fact, it was just a faint memory.

She was well and truly healed.

What she'd felt for Thomas had been real enough, but looking back, she realized it had faded over the last five years. So had the anger. Now there were just sweet memories.

If Thomas and Gina truly loved each other, if they were truly meant to be together, maybe it was better that Morgan had learned it then, rather than further down the road.

Maybe.

It was a thought to consider.

A thought that plagued her the rest of the day. She finally gave up pretending to work and decided to walk Gilligan.

During the school year, Oakland was crowded with college students from Carlow University, Pitt, Carnegie Mellon. The small section of Pittsburgh was filled with the prestigious universities and their students. But now, in early June on a bright Sunday evening, there were very few young people around. There was still hustle and bustle—four major hospitals, plenty of businesses, along with the Carnegie Museum, were all in the area. Despite the activity, the usual vitality seemed missing without all the college kids.

She tugged at the lead. "Come on, Gilligan, keep up." They started back home.

Home.

She realized that in just the short amount of time she'd been there, Uncle Auggie's house—a house that held so many happy memories for her—felt like home.

As if she'd come home.

Which was silly.

San Diego was her home now.

She had friends there, a life there.

Her time in Pittsburgh was just a short diversion. She wasn't home, just on a visit.

But that didn't mean she couldn't enjoy her time here, really make use of it.

Maybe she'd make peace with Gina and Thomas.

Today was a start, Morgan mused, but talking to Gina wasn't enough. Before she could really put the past to rest, she'd have to face Thomas. She knew it was about the last thing on earth she wanted to do, but she also knew it was one of the things she probably couldn't avoid.

All the self-help gurus talked about closure.

She was pretty sure that's what she'd achieved today with Gina. Now, all she had to do was confront Thomas and she could close the book on that chapter of her life.

Without realizing she'd made a decision, Morgan pulled her cell phone out of her pocket and flipped it open. "Hi, Sunny. I need Gina's address."

She thought about taking Gilligan home, but Gina and Thomas's house wasn't very far away. Not far at all. She decided to get this confrontation over with.

Even with Gilligan's less than speedy gait, she reached the small gray-sided house within a few minutes. Before she lost her nerve, she walked to the front door and knocked. Gilligan flopped to the ground in a state of exhaustion.

Gina opened the door, her surprise quite evident on her expression. "Morgan?"

Thomas followed her. "Morgan?" he echoed.

Morgan waited for the once familiar spurt of attraction, of love. But all she felt was...well, not much.

Oh, Thomas was okay looking, but he didn't even stir the ember of excitement that Mark had. There wasn't any hint of infatuation. Not a smidgen of lust. Just the same kind of glow she'd felt when she'd seen her old friends that first Sunday. A sense of familiarity, of happy recollections.

"Morgan?" Gina repeated.

"I just came to say I'm happy you two are happy. I grew up with you both. Gina, you were my best friend, and Thomas, you were a friend long before we… Before… Well, you were a friend, too. I'm just glad that you're happy, that things worked out."

"Morgan, we never meant—" Thomas began.

She held up her hand. "I know. And even when I was so hurt, I think I knew that by telling me, you were saving me from more pain later on. I'm not saying I think we can have what we once had, but I do think the three of us can find something new. And maybe we could start by Sunday brunches, Gina?"

Gina's face practically disappeared beneath her smile. "I'd like that. I'd like that a lot."

"Great."

"Would you like to come in?" Thomas asked.

Morgan shook her head. "Not today, but you could ask me again sometime, okay?" She started toward the porch stairs. "I'll see you next Sunday, Gina."

"Sunday," her old friend said.

Morgan tried to decide what it was she was feeling as she walked down the sidewalk, tugging on Gilligan's lead. She felt…light. Lighter than she'd felt in years.

"Come on, Gilligan, let's go home."

CHAPTER ELEVEN

E.J., you know that old saying about when it rains it pours? It's definitely true. I'm feeling more than a little soggy....

MORGAN HADN'T LISTENED TO the answering machine all weekend. She'd been too wrapped up on Saturday with the reception, her crashing friends and then her impromptu dinner with Conner.

Then there had been her aborted brunch this morning and her reconciliation with her friends...with her past.

She'd spent the afternoon going all zennish as she tried to sort out her feelings. She finally decided she felt good. Really good.

Optimistic about...well, everything.

And as if to prove her newfound optimistic attitude was the right one, fate sent her a sign.

She'd been so busy putting her past to rest that she'd forgotten to fret about the future, so it was Sunday night before she saw the answering machine blinking. Even then, it wasn't her anxious checking that caused her to look. It was merely that she was turning off the living room lights, getting ready to go to bed, when she noticed the light was blinking a merry beat next to the number four.

Blink.

Blink.

Blink.

Blink.

Four messages.

She was suddenly wide-awake.

Message number one. "Hi, Morgan, it's me."

She didn't need more than that to know "me" was E.J. Finally.

"Still down here. It'll be a couple more weeks until I get back. I don't know when I'll be near a phone again, but I'll call when I can. I know how you worry, so this is just to say I'm fine."

"Message number two," said the metallic voice.

"Hello. This is Ellie Marx calling for Morgan Miller. I have your résumé in front of me, and Turner, Inc. is very interested in an interview. Please call me at your earliest possible convenience at…"

Morgan grabbed a notepad and took down the number.

"Message number three."

"Ms. Miller, this is Jerry Johns, at Cameron and Peters here in San Diego. We'd like to fly you out as soon as possible for an interview…."

She scribbled down more information.

"Message number four."

"Morgan…it's me. I miss—"

Marvin. She hit Delete before his message ended. Marvin was well and truly past tense, even if he didn't seem to get it.

She concentrated on the other messages. E.J. was fine and she had job possibilities.

Two, to be exact.

Not that she was counting or anything.

Hell, yes, she was counting. Two responses to her queries.

One of the cats—she wasn't sure if it was Lovey or Thurston—came out from behind the couch and curled around her leg.

She froze, not wanting to scare it back into the shadows.

Gilligan had no such compunction. As if sensing its presence, he barked from somewhere in the house, and the cat disappeared again.

"Do you want to go out?" she called.

Gilligan continued barking.

Here she was, talking to a dog.

Was that worse—in a questionable-sanity sort of way—than talking to herself?

Morgan sat on the porch steps while Gilligan sniffed every blade of grass in the small front yard.

It was two in the morning, and the street was quiet, which felt strangely disconcerting, considering her mind was anything but.

Job offers and Y chromosomes.

She couldn't do anything about the job calls until morning.

That left men. Conner, Mark and even her almost forgotten ex.

Men.

They were the bane of her existence.

No, that wasn't true. Too many men to think about all at once, that was what was hard.

She'd been off the market so long she wasn't sure what to do with such a bountiful batch.

Marvin. Well, that was easy. He was in San Diego and she was here. No proximity, no worries. Although, if one of these job offers panned out, they'd be close again. Morgan would just have to see to it that Marvin understood they were over. Whether she was in San Diego or Pittsburgh, it was done.

Mark and Conner, however, were here, and—

Just then a car pulled up next door and her mother got out.

No. Her mother *slithered* out, then leaned back into the car and said something to the driver before getting out all the way.

The car pulled away as her mother started to walk up the flower-lined sidewalk to her front door.

"Late night, Mom?"

Her mother gave a yelp. "Morgan Elisabeth Miller, what on earth are you doing out here at this hour?"

"I just noticed I had messages, and there was good news. I was too jazzed to sleep. Besides, Gilligan wanted to come out. The better question is, where were you until 2:00 a.m.?"

Her mother didn't say a word. She didn't need to. Morgan could see she wasn't going to like the answer.

"Mom?"

"I was out."

"I can see that. With…?"

"Friends."

"Which friends? Where? You're being awfully vague, and that concerns me."

"Morgan Elisabeth Miller, I certainly don't have to answer to you as to my whereabouts. I'm the mother. You're the daughter. You never seem to remember that. Even as a little girl."

Her mother used her full name when she was trying to pretend to be outraged. The fact that she'd used it twice in the course of this short conversation made Morgan's mom-radar beep out of control.

Morgan, on the other hand, found using her mother's first name to be the most efficient way to get answers. "Annabelle."

"It was Paul. I met him at a wake yesterday. He called today and we went out."

Morgan immediately felt guilty for being suspicious. "Oh, Mom, I'm sorry."

"So am I," she muttered, not sounding overwrought with grief.

"Who passed away?"

"Uh. Well, about that," her mother said, her voice a little louder than was wise at 2:00 a.m. in a residential neighborhood.

"Shh," Morgan warned.

"Fine," Annabelle said a bit more softly. "So I crashed a wake last night. It's not like I meant to. I thought it was some sort of celebration. A birthday, maybe. I mean, who has a wake in the banquet room in a bar on a Saturday night?" Before Morgan could say anything, her mother added quickly, "And I promised no more reception crashing. Wakes weren't included in the promise. And it certainly seemed to me there would be men my age at a wake."

Morgan couldn't think of anything to say to that, so she simply settled for, "Mother."

"Don't worry. You don't have to ask me to promise not to crash wakes. I do it of my own free will. I've decided they're not the way to go. Everyone tends to be depressed."

"You went out with a widower?"

"Give me some credit. Paul wasn't the widower, just a distant cousin." Her mother snorted. "A widower? Why, I'd definitely be the rebound relationship then, and we all know that never ends well. As it was, Paul was not exactly what I'd call chipper. Now, if you're finished with the inquisition, I'm going in." She turned and walked across the lawn to her own front door. "Good night."

"Good night," Morgan echoed softly. She noticed the dog was standing patiently in front of her. "Let's go to bed, Gilligan."

Morgan realized she wouldn't be tossing and turning the rest of the night, worrying about men.

She would be worrying about her mother.

She wasn't sure which was worse.

CHAPTER TWELVE

E.J., I'm going out with my Remington Steele meets Donald Trump man tonight. He's taking me to one of the fanciest restaurants in Pittsburgh. I should be more excited. Maybe I'm just so excited about the job leads that they've overshadowed everything else? That must be it, because Mark is exactly the type of man I've been looking for....

MONDAY NIGHT, MORGAN FOUND herself seated in Falines across from Mark. They had a window table. The view of the city was astounding.

She kept reminding herself that this dinner was supposed to be business, pure and simple. But Mark seemed to be determined to make it something else... something more.

Morgan wasn't sure she wanted more with him.

Pursuing more than business with Mark wasn't exactly unethical, but she wouldn't want the fact that he was gorgeous, that he was the type of man she'd always been attracted to, that if Donald Trump and Pierce Brosnan had a child he would be B. Mark Jameson, to sway her recommendation to her mother.

She knew without asking that Annabelle would say go for it. The problem was, Morgan wasn't sure what *it* was, and even worse, what she wanted *it* to be.

They chatted through the appetizer. Well, not quite chatted. They were playing a verbal tug-of-war. He wanted date-type conversation, while she tried to keep things businesslike until she could decide just what she wanted.

"Did you look at the figures I sent?" she'd ask.

He'd just nod and say, "Isn't it a beautiful night?"

She'd counter with questions about his opinion of her growth projections. He'd comment on the city lights spread out below them.

By the time their entrées arrived, she was feeling a bit desperate. She didn't want to discuss the weather, the city lights or the new exhibit at the Carnegie Museum.

"I want—" she began, but he cut her off before she could add, *to talk about OCDR.*

"What is it you want, Morgan?" Mark took a bite of his pasta dish, turning the simple act into a sensual experience. The fork rose to his mouth as if in slow motion, and his lips closed around the bite languidly. As he leisurely removed the fork and began to enjoy the taste, his eyelids fell lower, his expression one of well-sated pleasure.

Morgan's mouth went dry and her mind went numb as she watched him.

"Morgan?" he finally asked, after he'd finished the bite. "What is it you want?"

Ah, the question. She pulled herself together. It was one she'd asked herself a lot recently. She felt no closer to an answer for Mark than she did for herself. "If I were a beauty pageant contestant, my answer would be world peace, but I don't think you meant the question quite that broadly. So I'd have to say, I'd really like to talk about your thoughts on the figures I've collected for you. I'd like to know what you would do with the business, if my mother decided to sell to you. What are your plans?"

"No, a beauty pageant answer wasn't what I had in mind, and although I do want to discuss those figures and my plans, I'm more interested in what you're searching for professionally. What are you looking for in a new job?"

Morgan realized that there was simply no hurrying Mark along. So she thought a moment about his question as she finished her bite of salmon. It was good, but she knew she wasn't displaying the kind of pleasure Mark had.

She swallowed, then answered, "Something like what I'm doing now at the OCDR. A challenge. Something new. Feeling like I'm making a difference. I don't think I'd realized how much that was lacking at my old job."

"I may have a solution. I brought you this." He pulled a number of folded papers from his inside jacket pocket. "I hope you'll give it consideration. I know it's not what you were planning, but I think it might prove to be beneficial."

She opened the file and saw a job description,

followed by a numerical figure that made her wonder if she needed glasses.

"What's this?"

"My offer. I think you'll find that it meets your criteria. It would be something new, a challenge, and your taking the job would make a difference to me."

He reached across the table and rested his hand on hers. "I'd really like the opportunity to work with you."

"Why? You don't know me."

"I've done some checking. I hope you don't mind, but I called San Diego and talked to your boss—"

"Ex-boss," she interjected.

"Ex-boss. He had nothing but praise for you. And I've seen the presentation you made for OCDR. I like that you're looking into other options. Your mother assures me that was all your idea. And…" He paused, his fingers lightly stroking her hand.

Morgan realized she wanted nothing more than to yank her arm back.

Why?

Here was a man who was offering her everything she'd ever wanted on a business level, and he'd made it plain that he was offering the potential for more than that. B. Mark Jameson was her ideal man. A button-down planner who valued her worth. That should be irresistibly appealing to her. And yet she was resisting quite easily.

She realized he was still talking.

"Pardon?"

"I just said that I hope you'll consider my offer."

"I have two interviews in San Diego next week—"

"I'm not asking for anything concrete, I just want to

be in the running. Why don't you come down to my office and I'll give you a tour? Maybe Saturday morning? It's quiet then, but you'll get an idea of what we're all about. I'll even treat you to breakfast after."

"We could talk about positions now," she suggested, hopefully sidestepping the running question.

He quirked his eyebrow—the left one—as he smiled.

She realized what she'd said and blushed, which made him laugh. "Let's table the position talk. Right now, I'm in a great restaurant with a beautiful woman. I'd like to concentrate on that."

"I think I might be dating someone else," she said, as bluntly and succinctly as she could.

"Pardon me if I seem like I'm prying, but you didn't sound very sure."

"Yes, I'm sure. I'm dating someone else."

"Are you engaged?" he countered, looking totally unconcerned as he twirled another bite of his pasta around his fork.

"No," she admitted.

"But you've talked about dating exclusively?"

She shook her head.

"So how long have you been dating this particular someone else?"

"Well, dating is such a specific sort of word. We haven't actually gone out on a real date, although he's cooking for me tomorrow night and we've kissed…"

Mark's fingers drummed the table as he studied her. Whatever he saw seemed to please him because he stopped drumming, smiled and said, "As a business man, what I'm hearing is that there have been negotiations, but no deal's been finalized."

"Well, no."

"So, we'll meet on Saturday and talk about both my job offer and the other kind of offer I'd like to make."

"Mark, I don't want to lead you on about either. I have interviews in San Diego next week and—"

"Let's leave off all business talk for the evening and just enjoy the sights and the company."

"But—"

"So, tell me about growing up with Annabelle as a mother...."

It was as if he knew the one subject that could carry them through the rest of the meal with no problem.

Even as Morgan regaled him with tales of her mother's exploits, she studied him.

She'd never been actively pursued by anyone...not like this. It was sort of flattering. Mark was exactly the kind of man she'd always wanted.

She remembered what her mother had said at Uncle Auggie's wake: *Sometimes what you think you want isn't what you want at all.*

Morgan had been so sure then. Sure of herself and of her career path. Sure of where she wanted her life to go.

Her promotion at work. Marvin. Her friends. Her life in San Diego.

Now?

She wasn't sure about anything. And mainly, she wasn't sure what she was going to do about it. About any of it.

Conner and Mark.

Job offers.

OCDR.

Morgan's party crashing mother and friends.

The only thing she was actually sure of was that for the first time, no amount of list making, no amount of planning, seemed to help her decide what to do next.

CHAPTER THIRTEEN

E.J., I feel as if I'm in *Gone With the Wind,* running around hollering "I don't know anything about birthin' no babies"…or caring for them, for that matter.

MORGAN LOOKED AT THE PILE of clothing on her bed. She felt as if she were back in high school getting ready for a big date. And that was absurd, because not only was she well beyond high school, this wasn't a big date.

It was merely dinner with Conner. His brother was going to be there, for Pete's sake.

She looked at the pile of clothes again.

This was ridiculous.

She surveyed herself again in the mirror.

Her jeans—her good jeans—a tank top and a casual blazer. Heels. Low heels, but heels.

Did it say casual dinner with a man you sort of worked with, had fibbed to and kissed twice?

No.

She reached for a light summer dress and held it up. Maybe this would be better.

She was interrupted by the doorbell.

Not just a polite ring, but a long string of incessant ones.

Morgan hurried out through the living room and into the small foyer. She opened the door and spotted Sunny holding a squirming baby.

"Sunny?"

"I planned on asking your mom, but she's not home. Could you watch Johnny? They just called and Mom's at St. Kathryn's Hospital. They think she had a heart attack, and I need to—"

Morgan stopped her. "Don't worry. We'll be fine, right, Johnny?" She held her arms out and found them filled with baby. A baby who didn't look at all convinced of his fineness in her questionable hands.

She tried to look more assured than she felt. "We're okay. Just worry about your mom."

Sunny made another trip into the house with a diaper bag that resembled an old-fashioned steamer trunk and a car seat.

"I'll be back as soon as I can."

Morgan could see Sunny's anxiety and felt helpless to ease it. "Don't worry. We'll be fine," she stated once again.

Before she could offer any other comforts, Sunny was hurrying to her car and Morgan was left staring at the small face peering up at her.

"Well…" she said, not sure what to do. She took the baby and the giant bag and went back into the living room, wondering where Annabelle could be. "Mom promised no more wake crashing, and she might be many things, but she doesn't go back on promises."

The baby gave her an odd, uncertain look.

She wasn't sure if he was unsure about her mother's whereabouts or about Morgan's ability to care for him.

"Mom doesn't lie, and I can handle a baby like you, so you can stop giving me that look. You're too young to have such a cynical nature. Your mother is the most optimistic person I know, and that kind of outlook has to be genetic."

Johnny Paterniti didn't appear to be convinced, nor the least bit optimistic.

As a matter of fact, his face started to crumple a bit. More than a bit.

"Hey, I used to babysit. We'll be fine," she told him. She didn't mention that she'd never babysat, much less held, a baby as young as he was.

Johnny didn't seem overly impressed with her résumé.

Gilligan walked into the room, sniffed the air, and then turned and walked back out. Morgan sniffed in turn, but didn't smell anything other than baby lotion.

"Well, that's good," she said, not sure if she knew how to change a diaper, and not ready to find out.

"So…"

Johnny's face crumpled further and he opened his mouth. She thought he was going to cry, but instead, he—

"Yurp."

—threw up on her jacket.

"This is why I didn't babysit infants. I guess I'll be changing again…changing both of us, by the look of things."

This time she didn't have time for a dressfest, so she grabbed another jacket to replace the stained one.

She amazed herself by managing to get Johnny changed as well. He still didn't look happy with her abilities. Instead, he looked as if he blamed her for the entire throw-up fiasco.

She was about to proclaim her innocence, when the two cats came into the room. They sniffed and, unlike Gilligan, seemed to like the way Johnny smelled.

And the baby's face uncrumpled and he wore a delighted smile as he cooed at the cats. While he was concentrating on them, Morgan hurriedly finished changing him. Then it occurred to her that she'd better call her date.

She sat on the floor next to Johnny, who was still talking baby-babble to the cats, and phoned Conner. "Something's come up."

"Don't tell me you're canceling. I cooked and nothing's burned."

"So far," a voice bellowed from the background.

"That was my very helpful baby brother, Ian," Conner told her. "He's just upset that he's got to wash the dishes, and this meal's taken a few more than normal."

Ian yelled again, something Morgan couldn't quite make out. Conner growled, and that was enough to make her chuckle.

"So far, huh? Is your brother implying that burning is part of your normal cooking style?"

"I refuse to answer that on the grounds it might incriminate me and give you yet another reason not to come. Speaking of reasons, what's the problem?"

Morgan looked down at the reason. "I have an unexpected guest."

"Bring her along," Conner said.

"Him."

"Him?" He paused a moment, then asked, "Should I be jealous?"

"I don't know. Are you?" She waited for his answer.

"I—"

Suddenly she didn't want to know, because she wasn't sure what she wanted to hear, so she blurted out, "He's under a year old. A friend had an emergency and I'm babysitting."

"Ah. I guess I don't need to get out another place setting?"

"No. No extra place setting."

"Great. Bring him along. You can babysit here as easily as there. And here has a homemade meal waiting."

"Thanks, Conner. We'll both be there soon."

Did "great" mean he would have been jealous and it was great that he wasn't? "Great," she muttered as she disconnected the call.

Johnny stopped smiling at the cats and gave her another one of his iffy looks.

"No more cookie tossing," she warned him as she put him into the car seat. While he was sitting in it, she made a hurried call to Sunny's cell phone and left Conner's Lawn Street address, just so she knew where Johnny was.

Morgan didn't mention the baby didn't seem inclined to cooperate. She'd try to thread his arm through a strap in his car seat and he'd jerk it in the opposite direction.

"Come on, Johnny."

The cats sat in the doorway, watching her attempt. She wondered why they'd finally decided to come out of the shadows. Maybe they were accepting her?

Accepting or not, they looked as doubtful as Johnny did about her abilities to work the straps of the seat. But finally she got him buckled in.

Morgan carried the car seat by the handle, after throwing the diaper bag over one shoulder, her small purse over the other. There was a severe weight discrepancy between the two, and she felt a bit like Quasimodo as she made her way to the car.

That's when she was presented with her first—second, if you counted getting thrown up on, which she did—hurdle. How on earth did the seat hook into the car?

Straps, clips…baby.

She suddenly wished for an engineering degree instead of her stupid M.B.A.

But somehow she muddled through, giving the seat a big yank just to be sure it was secure.

"Yoo-hoo, Morgan. Where're you going?" Annabelle called.

She turned and eyed her mother suspiciously. "I think a better question would be where are you going…or rather, where are you coming from?"

Annabelle was dressed beyond the nines and firmly into the tens, in a gown that glittered and sparkled, strappy little shoes and a matching purse. And her hair was done up in an elaborate style that screamed *fancy*.

Her mother gave her a chagrined little smile. "There was a small shinding at the country club. Very nice. Let me tell you, a good party planner makes all the difference."

"Party planner?" Morgan mused, an idea forming. "What if OCDR hired a party planner? It would certainly be in keeping with my expansion ideas."

"Yes," her mother agreed, then gently added, "but my idea is to sell, remember?"

"I get that you want to sell, that you don't want to be in charge, but it doesn't make sense to sell if you're financially shorting yourself. If you could expand the business, offer more services, cost-effective add-ons, maybe—"

She came to an abrupt halt. "Uh, Mom, I didn't know you were a member of the country club."

Annabelle didn't respond.

"Mom?

Still nothing.

"Annabelle?" She said her mother's name with just the right amount of exasperation.

Annabelle's guilt was written all over her face. "Fine. I'm not a member. But maybe I'm thinking about becoming one if you expand the store and make me rich. So I went to a party tonight to check out the club. I mean, I wouldn't want to join if it was less than adequate."

Morgan had years of experience reading between the lines, distinguishing the difference between what her mother said and what she meant. "You crashed. Don't bother denying it, I can see it in your face. I thought we agreed no more crashing?"

Morgan glanced down at the baby, who was squirming in the car seat. His face was all crinkled and he looked to be on the verge of crying.

"We agreed no more crashing wedding receptions or even wakes," Annabelle said. "This wasn't either. This was a country club function."

"You're splitting hairs, Mother."

"If I am they're about the only hair I've seen tonight. I mean, I don't think I've ever seen such a large group of aging, balding, paunchy men. At least there were some pretty boys at the reception, even if they were a bit too young for me. Here the men were stodgy, and their wives…!"

Morgan surveyed her mother's neon-pink, strapless, skintight dress. It didn't take much of an imagination to figure out the wives' opinion of her mother.

"Oh, Mom."

"Well, you don't have to worry. No more crashing at the country club. I promise."

"No more crashing at all," Morgan corrected.

Rather than agree or disagree, Annabelle peeked in the back of the car. "Why, hi, Johnny, honey."

There was no face-puckering. No puking. Just a snaggle-toothed grin as the baby burbled in welcome.

"So, you're babysitting? That's good. I've been worried about you. You need more socialization."

An idea occurred to Morgan. It was perfect. Her mom had been Sunny's first choice in babysitters, and now that she was home from her purloined party she was available. "Sunny's mom is in the hospital. They think she had a heart attack. So Sunny came to see if you'd babysit—"

"Oh, my," Annabelle exclaimed before Morgan could finish. "I'd better go be with her. She's so close to her mom. She must be worried sick."

And without another word, Annabelle turned around and hurried back to her car.

"She's at St. Kathryn's," Morgan called.

Annabelle waved without turning around.

"That's the thing about my mom," Morgan told the baby as she got into her seat and snapped her seat belt in place, with a lot more ease than she'd had with his. "Annabelle's got no sense of decorum, but she's all heart."

Johnny gurgled in agreement.

They drove across town to Lawn Street and started to scan the car-lined, narrow avenue for a parking place.

This wasn't the kind of neighborhood she expected Conner to live in. Oh, she didn't expect an Upper St. Clair address, but... She looked over at the small brick house.

Morgan didn't even try to get the car seat back out. She'd save that job for Sunny. Instead she unbuckled Johnny and unthreaded his limbs, then lifted him in her arms.

Morgan tried to find a comfortable way to hold the baby, his things, plus her purse, but didn't quite manage it. She was glad when she finally reached the house and rang the doorbell.

The door opened a moment later, but it wasn't Conner standing on the other side. Instead, there was a slimmer, younger version of him, wearing braces on his legs and leaning heavily on a set of crutches. A skin-toned bandage was plastered across his forehead.

"You must be Conner's brother," she said.

"Ian. Ian Danning. And you must be Morgan, Conner's new assistant, of sorts."

"Guilty as charged," she said, feeling guilty indeed.

He must have noticed her looking at his bandage, because he added, "You should see the other guy," then laughed. "And this is?"

"Johnny. A good friend's son. She got called into the hospital, and I'm babysitting."

Johnny let out a plaintive whine.

"And I don't think Johnny's all that impressed with visiting me," Morgan murmured.

"Come on in and let me give it a try. I'm great with kids."

The living room held an eclectic mix of furnishings that would have made any HGTV designer shudder. A ragged leather sofa, two mismatched armchairs, and an assortment of dented-looking lamps. A huge fireplace that had ashes left in it from the last fire... Yet the mishmash somehow came together to make a welcoming room.

Ian took a seat on the couch, tossed his crutches on the floor and held his hands out for the baby.

"You're sure?" Morgan asked.

"I worked my way through college as a nanny to three boys. I think I can manage."

Gladly, she handed Johnny over. "I don't think he likes me."

"He could tell you were tense. Babies sense things like that. Right, buddy?"

If babies truly did sense someone's tension, then it was obvious that Ian didn't have an ounce in him. A minute later Johnny was gurgling happily and bouncing on his legs as if they were old friends.

"I haven't had much experience with them," Morgan admitted, eyeing the contented baby.

"No kids. No wedding ring," Ian murmured, then looked up at her and grinned. "Not to make you nervous or anything, but I'm checking you out this evening. I know Conner says you're just a new colleague, but I don't know that I quite buy that story. It's been a long time since my brother's had a woman over."

What's Your Reading Pleasure...
ROMANCE? <u>*OR*</u> SUSPENSE?

Do you prefer spine-tingling page turners OR heart-stirring stories about love and relationships? Tell us which books you enjoy – and you'll get 2 FREE "ROMANCE" BOOKS or 2 FREE "SUSPENSE" BOOKS with no obligation to purchase anything.

Choose **"ROMANCE"** and get **2 FREE BOOKS** that will fuel your imagination with intensely moving stories about life, love and relationships.

FREE!

Choose **"SUSPENSE"** and you'll get **2 FREE BOOKS** that will thrill you with a spine-tingling blend of suspense and mystery.

FREE!

Whichever category you select, your 2 free books have a combined cover price of $11.98 or more in the U.S. and $13.98 or more in Canada.

And remember... just for accepting the Editor's Free Gift Offer, we'll send you 2 books and a gift, ABSOLUTELY FREE!

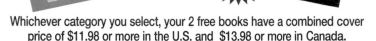

YOURS FREE! *We'll send you a fabulous surprise gift absolutely FREE, just for trying "Romance" or "Suspense"!*

® and ™ are trademarks owned and used by the trademark owner and/or its licensee.

Order online at
www.FreeBooksandGift.com

Offer limited to one per household and not valid to current subscribers of MIRA, Romance, Suspense or "The Best of the Best." All orders subject to approval. Books received may vary. Credit or debit balances in a customer's account(s) may be offset by any other outstanding balance owed by or to the customer. Please allow 4 to 6 weeks for delivery.

YOUR READER'S SURVEY "THANK YOU" FREE GIFTS INCLUDE:

▶ 2 Romance OR 2 Suspense books

▶ A lovely surprise gift

PLEASE FILL IN THE CIRCLES COMPLETELY TO RESPOND

1) What type of fiction books do you enjoy reading? (Check all that apply)
- ○ Suspense/Thrillers
- ○ Action/Adventure
- ○ Modern-day Romances
- ○ Historical Romance
- ○ Humour
- ○ Science fiction

2) What attracted you most to the last fiction book you purchased on impulse?
○ The Title ○ The Cover ○ The Author ○ The Story

3) What is usually the greatest influencer when you <u>plan</u> to buy a book?
- ○ Advertising ○ Referral from a friend
- ○ Book Review ○ Like the author

4) Approximately how many fiction books do you read in a year?
○ 1 to 6 ○ 7 to 19 ○ 20 or more

5) How often do you access the internet?
○ Daily ○ Weekly ○ Monthly ○ Rarely or never

6) To which of the following age groups do you belong?
○ Under 18 ○ 18 to 34 ○ 35 to 64 ○ over 65

YES! I have completed the Reader's Survey. Please send me the 2 FREE books and gift for which I qualify. I understand that I am under no obligation to purchase any books, as explained on the back.

Check one:

| **ROMANCE** |
| 193 MDL EE3V   393 MDL EE37 |

| **SUSPENSE** |
| 192 MDL EE4K 392 MDL EE4V |

FIRST NAME   LAST NAME

ADDRESS

APT.#   CITY

STATE/PROV.   ZIP/POSTAL CODE

◀ **DETACH AND MAIL CARD TODAY!** ▶

(SUR-SS-06) © 1998 MIRA BOOKS

The Reader Service — Here's How It Works:

Accepting your 2 free books and gift places you under no obligation to buy anything. You may keep the books and gift and return the shipping statement marked "cancel." If you do not cancel, about a month later we'll send you 3 additional books and bill you just $5.24 each in the U.S., or $5.74 each in Canada, plus 25¢ shipping & handling per book and applicable taxes if any.* That's the complete price and — compared to cover prices starting from $5.99 each in the U.S. and $6.99 each in Canada — it's quite a bargain! You may cancel at any time, but if you choose to continue, every month we'll send you 3 more books, which you may either purchase at the discount price or return to us and cancel your subscription.

*Terms and prices subject to change without notice. Sales tax applicable in N.Y. Canadian residents will be charged applicable provincial taxes and GST.

"Really?"

"Really," Ian assured her. "So of course it's up to me to see to it you're on the up-and-up. Conner's out of practice attending to that sort of thing himself."

"What am I out of practice on?" Conner asked as he walked into the room.

"Women," Morgan said, smiling at him. "Your brother's afraid I'm some sort of vamp who will take advantage of you."

"I can only hope. You have my permission to take any advantages you want," Conner assured her, as he leaned over and lightly kissed her cheek. "And who is this?"

"My friend Sunny's son, Johnny." The baby babbled a string of happy syllables, then smacked at Ian's face, laughing hard, as if he'd done something marvelous. "I think he likes Ian."

"Ian has a way with kids…and women. So watch out. He might say he's checking you out for me, but he's probably just checking you out."

"Well, she is rather checkable," Ian joked.

Something buzzed loudly from the direction Conner had come.

"Entertain her," Conner told Ian. "But don't be too entertaining. I've got to baste." He hurried back down the hall.

"He's cooking something that needs to be basted?" Morgan asked. "I'm impressed. My best cooking comes in the form of a bag with some nice restaurant's logo printed on it."

"He's gone all-out," Ian assured her. "And I was only half joking when I said it had been a long time. He hasn't had a woman over since he broke up with his last girlfriend. Or rather, she broke up with him."

"How long ago was that?" Morgan found herself asking. It shouldn't matter, because whatever she ended up having with Conner could only be temporary. Who they'd been with before didn't—couldn't—matter.

Keep it superficial, she warned herself. "Never mind, forget I asked."

"No, I like that you care. It's been almost two years now. Right after my accident. His ex didn't like that he was taking so much time with me."

"I'm sure—" Morgan started to protest.

Ian cut her off. "I'm sure as well. Oh, that's not what she said, but that's why." He nodded at his crutches. "Conner put his relationship, his job, his whole life on hold for me. I just thought I should tell you he's the real deal. And if you hurt him..."

"I don't think we've reached a point where I could hurt him. I'm not even sure if you can call this a date."

"It's a date," Ian assured her.

"I don't know. I mean, just because a man and a woman dine together, that doesn't make it a date. I have a friend back in San Diego, a guy. We've eaten together countless times, and it's never once been a date."

"I don't know if I believe a man and woman can be just friends."

"E.J. and I are. That's all we've ever been, all we'll ever be. No hope of anything more, but that's fine by both of us. We're just very good friends."

Ian still didn't look as if he was buying it.

"We met when I went to the emergency room with stomach flu. I introduced myself by throwing up on his shoes. Once you've done that, there's no chance you'll ever date."

"Have you thrown up on Conner's shoes?" Ian asked.

"No."

"Then it's a date. He's making a roast, and there's crème brûlée for dessert. Crème brûlée is only for dates. I assure you that in the couple years we've been living together, he's never made it for just the two of us. It's date food."

Morgan felt a momentary pang of discomfort, but Ian's smile disarmed her. "So, it's definitely a date," she said.

He nodded.

"Well, then whatever happens after, I can promise I'll try not to hurt him."

"That's all I ask."

Johnny gave a squawk and Ian joggled him. "I think it's safe to say this guy doesn't like being ignored."

Morgan noted the ease with which Ian handled the baby. She was impressed, and obviously, so was Johnny, who was beaming up at his new hero.

"Who's ignoring what?" Conner asked as he reentered the room.

"Morgan and I were just chatting and Johnny didn't like being less than the center of attention."

"Well, dinner's served." Conner held out a small, plastic bowl. "And since I don't think Johnny's up for eating roast, I found some Cheerios for him."

"Do babies eat Cheerios?" Morgan asked.

"How old is he?" Ian countered. "Almost a year?"

"Eleven months, I think," she said.

"Then yes, it's fine. He's got a couple teeth and should be able to handle Cheerios."

"You know, Ian, you should think about doing this

professionally. You're good." Morgan was pretty sure that he couldn't handle a baby and his crutches, too, so she said, "How about I carry him out to the dining room?"

Ian didn't appear to be the least bit insulted as he handed Johnny over. The baby turned to see who had him, and when he saw it was Morgan, he squawked in displeasure.

"See? He doesn't like me. Ian, you do have a way with babies."

"Too bad it wasn't babes," Conner teased. "Now, me…" He left the statement hanging.

"Yeah, you." Ian laughed as he sat down and took Johnny on his lap again. But then the doorbell rang.

Moments later, Conner came back into the dining room, Sunny at his heels.

"How's your mom?" Morgan asked by way of a greeting.

"She'll be fine. Turns out it wasn't a heart attack, it was indigestion. A bad case of indigestion. A few antacid tablets and a suggestion that she see her own doctor, and she was done. I dropped her off at home and came to get Johnny. I'm so sorry to have interrupted your plans. We'll just—"

"Take a breath," Morgan told her friend. "And let me make introductions. Ian and Conner Danning, this is Johnny's mother, Sunny Paterniti."

"I believe this young man belongs to you," Ian said, as Johnny wiggled and bounded in his arms, gurgling a greeting to his mother.

"Please sit down and join us," Conner said. "I'll get you a plate."

"Really, I'm fine. I'll just take Johnny and get out of your way."

"I know what it's like to get that kind of call," Conner said softly. "I'm going to bet you didn't eat."

"It's best not to argue," Ian told Sunny. "You might not be able to tell from his big, tough-guy exterior, but inside, my big brother is a nurturer."

"Really?" Morgan asked. "Do tell."

"Oh, the stories I know," Ian assured her. "Why, there was the time—"

"Morgan," Conner said, interrupting his brother. "Why don't you come out to the kitchen with me and help me get Sunny a place setting."

Ian laughed. "I think my brother wants to maintain his tough facade and not give you too many clues about his cookie-dough center."

"Come on, Morgan," Conner said, practically dragging her from the dining room."

"So, a big tough guy like you can't carry a place setting by yourself?" Morgan teased, trying to cover the fact that being this close to him was affecting her.

"That's not why I asked you out here," he assured her, his voice low and inviting.

Too inviting.

She took a step closer. "It's not?"

"No. You see, I've been wondering since you arrived what it would be like to kiss you again. And I thought if we snuck away for a minute I might find out if it's as good as I remember."

Thinking of Ian's warning, Morgan decided they'd better set some ground rules. "Conner, I'm only here for a short while longer. I have a few interviews set up in San Diego next week and…" She sighed. "I just don't want any confusion. I like you. A lot. But I will be leaving."

"My life is on the cusp of changing as well. As much as I like you, I'm leaving town as soon as Ian's settled in his new place."

"So, we're agreed we won't let it be more than it is. Two people at a crossroads, sharing a few good times together."

"Agreed," Conner said, taking her hand as if to shake on it, but instead, raising it to his lips and caressing it, before pulling her to him. "I haven't been able to think of anything but kissing you again since I left your place Saturday night."

With that pronouncement, he did just what he'd said he'd been thinking about. Those first two kisses had been wonderful, but this was more.

This was carnal.

It was more than just a kiss, it was a prelude of what they could have together.

"Wow," Morgan breathed. "Could I convince you to do it again?" she asked, feeling bold. Feeling sure of herself.

"Yes, but first I think we'd better get that place setting out to your friend."

DINNER WITH CONNER WAS AS casual as the previous evening's meal with Mark had been formal. Morgan couldn't remember when she'd laughed so much. And Sunny seemed to have just as good a time.

After they'd all lingered over dessert, Ian offered to walk her friend out to the car. Morgan noticed that he was watching Sunny intently, as if he expected her to say she could manage by herself, but instead, she suggested, "Why don't you get the diaper bag, and I'll get the baby, oh, and the carseat from Morgan's car."

Conner started cleaning up the remnants of the impromptu dinner party, and it seemed only natural for Morgan to offer to help. Ian popped his head into the kitchen, all smiles and said good-night, yawning for emphasis as he walked down the hall.

"I don't think your brother was as tired as he let on," Morgan said.

"No. He's just smart enough to realize I want you all to myself."

"I think he really hit it off with Sunny."

"There were some definite sparks there," Conner said.

"Ian was right."

"About?"

"Under that tough-guy facade, you're a nurturer, a marshmallow, a closet matchmaker."

"I…he…" Conner sputtered.

Morgan laughed. "It's sexy."

His demeanor immediately changed from indignant to interested. "Oh? Do tell."

"Very sexy."

"Are you by any chance hitting on me, Miss Miller?"

"That's Ms. Miller. And yes, Mr. Danning, I believe I am."

He sat on the couch and crooked his finger. "Then come over here and let me show you that not everything about me is soft."

She laughed as she obliged. "Do you know what I like about you, Conner?"

"My manly good looks? My incredible talent with a

camera?" He stopped. "Come on, jump in and give me your list."

"I like that you make me laugh. I don't know that I've ever been this turned on by someone and found myself laughing. It's nice."

"Laughing with you is nice, but I can think of something else I'd like to do with you."

"Your brother…?"

"Sleeps like a log. Plus he's at the back of the house on the first floor, and my room's at the front of the house on the second floor."

"So it would be private."

"Very."

Morgan thought about Mark, about job offers and interviews, about the fact that she'd be heading back to San Diego as quickly as she could. About all the reasons she should say no to his obvious proposal. Then she thought about her reaction to him, about how her body had already told him yes. "I think I'd—"

A sharp knock at the door interrupted her.

"Who could that be?" Conner asked.

Morgan followed him to the door.

Sunny stood in the stoop, looking worried. "Morgan, your mother's been trying to get hold of you."

"I've got my cell phone." Morgan grabbed her purse off the stand next to the door, pulled it out and flipped the lid. "Dead battery. Sorry. What's up?"

"Your mom…she's being held by security at the hospital and needs you to come get her."

CHAPTER FOURTEEN

"MOTHER, I CAN'T BELIEVE YOU... How could you..."

Annabelle had listened to Morgan sputter sentence fragments since they'd gotten into the car. She decided it was in her best interest to just wait until her daughter ran out of words.

"I mean, at your age—"

At your age?

All thoughts of simply waiting out the storm evaporated.

At your age?

Those were fighting words.

Annabelle didn't feel as if there was anything wrong with her age. She was in her prime. But obviously Morgan felt otherwise.

"Stop the car, I forgot my walker back at the hospital."

"What?" Morgan was slow on the uptake tonight.

"'At your age!'" Annabelle mocked. "I'll have you know I haven't signed up for Medicare just yet."

"I never said you had, but Mom—"

"And last time I checked, I was in complete control of my financial, spiritual and mental health."

"Mom, I didn't mean—"

"I don't act old. I saw a psychic once who said I have a young soul. But you, on the other hand, were born with a geriatric one."

"Mom, we're not going to argue about whose soul is older. We're going to discuss your crashing problems like sane, rational adults."

"I didn't crash anything. I just borrowed a coat."

"You stole a lab coat."

"That party dress wasn't exactly warm. I think whoever sets the air-conditioning unit at the hospital suffers from hot flashes. They're the old ones you should be worrying about."

"Mom, you went to the hospital for a noble reason, to be there for Sunny and her mom. But you couldn't help yourself, could you? You're addicted to crashing. When you saw the opportunity, you took it. You went trolling for a doctor. You and I both know it. You went to be with Sunny, then just…broke in. Mom, you crashed a hospital."

"But I didn't crash a reception, a wake or even a country club." She'd promised not to attend those particular gatherings and she hadn't.

"And you parked in a handicapped space at a hospital. Your car got towed. Then you were picked up by hospital security for impersonating a doctor."

Annabelle did feel guilty for the parking situation.

She'd been so anxious to get to Sunny that she'd simply taken the first open spot she'd come to. She hadn't even noticed the sign. Annabelle Miller was many things— things her daughter didn't approve of—but she was not a habitual handicapped-parking-space thief. She'd always felt people like that were the lowest of the low.

Morgan took a deep breath. "What's going on with you, Mom?"

Annabelle had a long litany of excuses and explanations she could offer, but instead opted for honesty. "I'm lonely."

That brought Morgan's lecture to an abrupt halt. Annabelle saw the wave of pity cross her daughter's face, and it cut at her. She didn't want Morgan feeling sorry for her. "I'm lonely, but I'm dealing with it in a proactive manner. I'll be fine."

"Mom, I'm sorry. I was gone a long time, but I'm here now."

"And it's wonderful having you home, but how long will it last? You've made it clear that you want to go back to San Diego, to the life you've built there. Then where will I be? It's not that I blame you. I'm your mother and I want you to be happy. You need to live your own life. But your father's gone, Auggie's gone and you're going again. Where does that leave me?"

"You have friends."

"But it's not the same as family, not the same as having someone to go to bed with, to wake up with. I'm lonely, Morgan. It's that simple. Crashing that first reception with you shook me out of my complacency."

"I'm sorry. I've been selfish. I'll try—"

"No, you haven't been selfish. You're living your

own life, finding your own way. That's all I've ever wanted for you."

Morgan laughed. "That's all? Then what was with all the come-home phone calls?"

"Okay, so maybe I wish you'd find your way back here to Pittsburgh. But even if you did, if you stayed and made your life here, I'd still want you to find someone."

"Mom, I know you think I don't understand, but I do. I think most people want a partner, someone to share their lives with. And you've been on your own a long time. I'm happy you're getting back into dating." Morgan paused. Annabelle could sense she was weighing her words. "I won't ask you not to look, but while you're at it, would you mind not impersonating any more doctors?"

Annabelle was impressed that Morgan wasn't trying to get her to swear off party crashing altogether. Maybe there was hope for her daughter, after all. "I can promise you that much."

"Or police officers, federal agents, judges… Let's just try and keep your search legal, okay?"

"I promise." Annabelle looked across the car at Morgan. Even though it was dark, she knew her daughter's every feature, every expression. She didn't need to see her clearly to know that right now she was looking exasperated and sympathetic all at once. "Morgan, in case I haven't mentioned it, I'm glad you're here, for however long."

"You know what, Mom? Me, too."

They rode in silence, each of them lost in thought. Annabelle went from worrying about Morgan finding her way, to wondering if that was hypocritical, since she herself had yet to figure her own life out.

Whether she should keep or sell the store, and most importantly whether she'd ever find a special someone of her own.

CHAPTER FIFTEEN

E.J., home might be where the heart is, but work…that's where the fun is. I always loved tackling new projects at LM Co., but at the Chair and Dish there's even more to do, and I'll confess, I'm enjoying doing it….

MORGAN WAS BACK AT THE office the next morning, a little worse for wear because of her late night out. Strangely, being a bit tired didn't dim her spirits. She felt as if she was back on track. She felt invigorated, ready to tackle anything.

She spent the day straightening out her mother's accounts, and felt she made huge inroads. After their talk, she felt as if she had Annabelle straightened out, too. Well, at least as straightened out as Annabelle could be.

Morgan could hear Sunny at the front desk humming

a happy tune. Obviously, a late night hadn't dimmed her spirits, either.

Morgan peeked through the door that separated the back office from the front counter. "Someone's been in a good mood all day."

Johnny, who'd come to work with Sunny since his grandmother was still recovering from her trip to the hospital and had begged off babysitting, scowled at her.

Scowled.

It wasn't right that he knew how to make that rather disgusted expression at under a year old.

"And I wasn't talking to you, Johnny," Morgan muttered. Sunny laughed and Morgan felt obliged to point out, "He really doesn't like me. Did you see how he looked at me? And after he barfed on me and everything. Some gratitude."

"You're imagining things. He likes you a lot, don't you, Johnny?" Sunny cooed, lifting the baby in her arms. He laughed for his mother, but Morgan could have sworn he shot her a smug look.

"He loves you, my Johnny does," Sunny assured her. "He's just a bit shy with strangers."

"He wasn't shy with Ian."

"Well, Ian's…well, he's Ian." Sunny blushed.

Morgan ignored the grim-faced baby and focused on his pink-cheeked mother. "He is, is he?"

"What's that supposed to mean?"

"Oh, Ian, you set my little heart pattering," Morgan exclaimed in a high falsetto.

Sunny went from pink to beet-red in a split second. "I never said that."

"No, but he did set your heart to pitter-pattering. I can

tell. You liked him." She switched to a schoolgirl's singsong voice and added, "Sunny's got a boyfriend."

"I don't." Sunny suddenly refocused, narrowed her eyes and said, "But you do."

"Nonsense. I'm just working with Conner. Last night was a business dinner."

"What about the other one, the night before? Mark? He did, after all, send you flowers this morning."

"That was simply to woo me into convincing Mom that selling to him is a good plan."

"Is it?"

"His offer seems on the up-and-up, but something feels off. I just can't put my finger on what. But I'll figure it out."

"Maybe you're attracted to him, and it's clouding your opinion of the business deal?"

Morgan didn't think that was it. She chatted with Sunny a few more minutes, then headed into the office.

Mark's offer was just one more thing think about, to decide. She'd figured her visit home in Pittsburgh would be downtime, but she felt busier than ever. It was probably good that she had those interviews in San Diego next week.

Morgan realized abruptly that she hadn't thought *home in San Diego*. Of course it was home. She missed it. Missed the ocean. Missed E.J.

Missed… What else did she miss?

Her job?

Not really. It had started to feel a bit boring. Same old, same old, different day.

But a new job, a new challenge would take care of that. And there was so much she wanted to get done before she left. She was going to bring OCDR, and her mother, kicking and screaming into the new millennium.

Speaking of kicking and screaming, as if on cue Annabelle came into the back and eyed the boxes suspiciously. "What is all that?"

"That is your new computer system. I have two more terminals that I'll pick up next week and install at the front desk, and one at the warehouse."

"We don't need—"

Morgan cut her off. "You do need. The store does need. Whether you keep OCDR as is, expand it or sell it, you need to update to stay competitive. Having a working computer system integrating all aspects of the business will make things more efficient if you keep it, or just add to the store's value if you sell."

"Morgan."

"Annabelle."

Her mother shook her head. "You always were unwavering when you'd decided something. That was it. The way it was. No one could convince you otherwise. It made you an unbelievably trying child."

"I guess it's a case of the apple not falling far from the tree, because you were an equally trying parent." Morgan smiled. "Do you have time for a lesson?"

"I'd love to, but I can't. I have a date soon. I know I just got in, but I only wanted to drop off this new order."

"A date with?"

"Was that the bell on the front door?" Annabelle cocked her head as if she'd heard something. "I'd better go check."

"Annabelle?"

"Fine. If you must know, yes, I have a date with a

man I met at the golf tournament last week. He called this morning."

"Since when do you golf, and what golf tournament?"

"At the club. I know I said I was done with it, that the men were way too old, or married, or both. But I decided to give it one more try."

"At least the odds are you won't be picked up by security."

Sunny popped her head in. "Morgan, you have a visitor."

Mark came into the office and clearly offered her his best smile. "Hi, Morgan."

Annabelle looked from Morgan to Mark, then back again. "Well, I'll just let you two get on with business. I have a date."

"But, Mom—" It was too late. Annabelle made a dash for the door and didn't look back.

Hoping against hope that her mom wouldn't break any laws while on her date, Morgan turned her attention to Mark. "So, what can I do for you?"

"I can think of any number of things, but let's start with you going out with me." On a tangent, he asked, "Did you like the flowers?"

"They were nice. Beautiful, in fact. Thank you. And as for going out, I really want to finish hooking this computer up."

"Everyone needs to eat." He moved closer.

She took a step back.

"I brought yogurt and a banana from home."

"That's not a meal, that's a snack." He took two more steps in quick succession and was right in front of her. "Speaking of snacks, before we go—"

"I haven't agreed to—"

"—I'd like to suggest we try a little snack of our own." And without a by-your-leave or do-you-mind, he kissed her.

It was a nice kiss. Maybe his technique was a bit too practiced. Nice, neat. Not too pushy, but not wimpy. Yes, it was nice.

Those three "nices" were fairly damning. Because, truth be told, she wanted more than nice when she was kissed. She wanted...

Conner Danning walked into the room just as Morgan pulled away from Mark.

"Sunny said to come back." He looked at Mark.

Mark looked at him.

Morgan looked from one to another as Conner introduced himself. "Conner. Conner Danning." He thrust out his hand.

"B. Mark Jameson." Mark took his hand.

There was a moment when Morgan expected a television sitcom type pissing war over whose grip was harder. But they let go in an almost civilized amount of time.

Almost.

"I just came to see if you'd like to do an early dinner." Conner cast a sideways glance at Mark. "Business. We need to talk about Friday's wedding."

"I came to ask the same question. And just like you, I thought we could combine business with pleasure. I'm buying the Chair and Dish Rental."

"You *want* to buy the store," Morgan corrected, stepping between them. "My mother hasn't decided whether she's keeping things status quo, expanding— which is what Conner's so graciously helping me research—or selling, which is what you're helping me explore."

Both men stared at each other, then looked expectantly at Morgan. "As for dinner..." She desperately tried to think of some Solomonlike solution.

She studied them. Conner in his white T-shirt and jeans, Mark in his designer suit. Both were good-looking...okay, beyond good-looking. They were—

"Morgan?" Mark said, nudging her from her thoughts.

"I..." She didn't know what to say and was relieved when the phone rang.

"Pardon me a moment. I've been waiting for a call about my flight to San Diego on Tuesday." She found the phone under a mass of packing foam from the computer components. "Hello?"

"Morgan, it's me, Nikki." Morgan didn't reply. She couldn't have. Nikki didn't take a breath, but just rushed on. "I was wondering if you'd like to go out? I have passes to—"

Salvation. Morgan didn't care what Nikki had in mind, she just knew that she had a way out of the dual invitations. She didn't wait for Nikki to finish. "Yes," she stated.

"Don't you want to know more about what?"

"No. Just the place and time."

Nikki blurted out the address. "Be there in an hour?"

"Great. Bye."

Morgan turned around and faced the two men, who were chatting semi-politely. "Sorry, guys. I appreciate both invitations, but I have plans. That was my friend Nikki, just firming them up. So, if you don't mind..." She started ushering them both toward the front of the shop. "I have to get home and get ready."

"Maybe I can have a raincheck? We do have a lot of business to discuss." Mark eyed Conner.

"We do as well," Conner added.

"Yes to both of you. I leave on Tuesday, but I hope to have all my recommendations for Mom ready by then, so yes, I do need to talk to both of you. But for right now, I have to run. A friend and I have big plans."

Morgan watched as, once outside, the two men turned and walked away in opposite directions.

"Problems?" Sunny asked.

"I don't know." It suddenly hit her that she'd said yes to Nikki without knowing what she'd agreee to. "I hope not."

CHAPTER SIXTEEN

E.J., with friends like Nikki, who needs enemies? Actually, you could say, with friends like Nikki, who needs a probation officer? The answer would be me.

FOUR HOURS LATER, MORGAN WAS sitting in the passenger seat of her mother's car.

They'd been riding in silence for the last few minutes—minutes that felt like hours.

The atmosphere was thick and heavy as Morgan waited, steeling herself for a well-deserved lecture. "Are you going to say anything?"

"Did you…"

Here it was—her mother's big lecture. It was bound to be a good one. To be honest, Morgan deserved nothing less than a lengthy tongue-lashing. She leaned closer to her mother's side of the car, almost anticipating the diatribe that was bound to come.

"…have a good time?"

"That's it? That's my lecture? Did I have a good time?" Morgan knew her mom had never been conventional. But she'd had to leave her own date in order to pick up her daughter from the police station, and all she could ask was if Morgan had a good time?

"Well, what's the point of a good exploit if you don't enjoy it?" Annabelle asked in her most reasonable tone.

"I didn't plan for this evening to turn into an exploit. When Nikki called and asked me out, I had two crazy men in my office, which is the only reason I jumped at her offer to go to a party. I should have been suspicious when she said Tessa had declined the invitation, but she pinned an ID tag on my dress and maneuvered me into the reception hall before I got out more than a quick hello. I just figured her invitation had something to do with her working at the paper. And I'll admit, the party didn't seem too bad—well, up until the point that the real owners of those IDs showed up and made a stink."

"But you had a good time before that." It was a statement, not a question.

"Mom, I was held for questioning by the police. This is your turn to lecture me. Tell me how irresponsible I was, how much trouble I could have gotten into if it wasn't for Nikki's fast talking."

"Honey, I've never had to lecture you because you do such a great job of it on your own. You worry, you agonize, you angst. You nitpick everything, wondering what you could have done differently, what you could have done better. You've never needed my help at berating yourself. You're a pro."

"Maybe this time I need some outside criticism. I mean, I crashed another party—this one at the Pittsburgh Regional Security Conference. Law enforcement from all over the area were there for a three-day seminar. They seemed to take offense that the security for their security meeting was so easily compromised. I think they'd have preferred that it had been for some nefarious reason instead of two women trolling for dates."

"But Nikki talked to that nice officer and explained the situation. Not only are you off the hook, but she's *got* a date."

"But—"

"Morgan, you can't worry about what might have happened. You just have to deal with what is. And the reality is this was nothing. Nikki got a date, you're on your way home with me. By the way, why didn't *you* get a date?"

"I wasn't looking for a date. I have too many men in my life as it is. Conner and Mark are both interested. And Marvin wants to de-ex himself, but being in San Diego, he's the least of my man problems."

"Morgan, honey, a woman can never have too many men." Annabelle tsked. "I thought I'd taught you better than that."

Despite her best intentions, Morgan chuckled. But the flash of humor didn't last long. She sighed. "I'm such a mess. I feel as if I'm standing on the brink of something, but I'm not sure what. Mark and Conner, Conner and Mark?"

"Enjoy the moment with each and trust that it will all come out right in the end."

"I guess, in the end, it doesn't matter. I have one more wedding with Conner this weekend. And I started doing some digging on Mark's company on my own, as well as studying his proposal. I should have some solid information and suggestions for you next week before I leave. Hopefully, I'll come back from my trip with a new job, and all this worry will be over."

"That's what you want? To go back to San Diego?"

"Of course it's what I want. It's what I've been working and planning for."

"But is it what you really want or what you think you want? There's a difference."

CHAPTER SEVENTEEN

"So, how was your night out with your friend?" Conner asked Morgan by way of a salutation two evenings later at the Ross and Antoske wedding.

"I'd rather not talk about it." Her expression said what she didn't—that it hadn't gone well.

"Oh. And that Mark? Did you two ever get together and discuss him buying the store?"

Grilling Morgan about her dinner with another guy wasn't how Conner intended to start the evening.

No, he'd planned to play it cool, as if seeing Morgan with another man hadn't fazed him in the least.

And of course, it hadn't.

After all, they'd both agreed that getting serious wasn't in the cards for either of them. It just wouldn't be practical.

Practical and cool. Those were his watchwords.

Yet the moment Morgan climbed into his car, the words he hadn't been going to say popped out. He might have groaned over how juvenile the question sounded if she wasn't sitting there, looking at him as if he'd grown horns.

He forced his focus back onto the road.

"Pardon?" she finally said.

He flipped on his turn signal and changed lanes, not that there was any need, but simply because it gave him something to do. "I just wondered how your meeting went with that guy who wants to buy your mother's business."

What he really wanted to ask was just what kind of business she had with Mark, but there was no way to do that and not sound jealous. And, of course, he wasn't jealous.

Time to change the subject. "Speaking of business, an old friend called with a lead for me."

"That's great. You must be so excited. I know I am about these interviews in San Diego next week," she said, then started rhapsodizing about the city itself, about southern California and the life she had there.

Conner listened, but realized she hadn't answered his question about that Mark guy. And maybe by not answering she was giving him an answer, after all.

ALL THE WAY TO THE RECEPTION Morgan continued to give her best Pollyanna impersonation about her trip to San Diego, yet she felt anything but upbeat and optimistic. Conner's news about a job lead disturbed her. Sure, she was happy for him, but she didn't want their time to draw to a close just yet.

To be honest, she'd been in a funky mood ever since she and her mother parted company the other night. Her mom's question about whether she really wanted to go back to San Diego or just thought she did rankled.

Everything rankled.

Her mother's crashing private parties and other events rankled, not to mention her newfound sage sayings.

Morgan almost getting arrested, but not getting a date, rankled.

Not wanting a date with anyone except Conner rankled…except maybe with Mark.

Best not forget her newfound indecisiveness—it definitely rankled. That wasn't like her. Not like her at all. Morgan always had a plan.

She realized she was scratching her neck. The tag on her shirt was rubbing it raw, and she added it to her list of aggravations, along with the fact that today's bride had dressed her bridesmaids in gowns even worse than the pink monstrosity Morgan had been forced to wear. And the fact that that bothered her was puzzling. After all, she wasn't wearing one of the puce dresses. But in the interest of bridesmaids throughout the world, she was put out. She understood brides wanted to outshine everyone, even their closest friends and relatives, but still, there was outshining and then there was just being sadistic.

The pink dress had been a case of the bride wanting to shine.

These puce ones were sadistic, and looking at them just intensified Morgan's dark mood. After all, itchy tags and sadistic brides were much easier to think about than all the other things that kept flitting through her mind.

This particular funk and its accompanying list were getting her nowhere fast. She had to get down to business. So, what other items could OCDR stock to rent or to sell?

They were well into the reception and she already had a rather impressive collection of items to check into.

The long white runner the bride walked down. Could they rent them? How difficult would the upkeep and cleaning be? Would there be a large enough profit margin?

The bride and groom's cake servers, the special champagne glasses. And though this reception was in a hall, what about a few tents? Pavilions?

Her mind was racing as she passed out disposable cameras, stopping every so often to jot down more notes.

Making a list, especially a long one, lightened her mood from black to a dark shade of gray. Morgan managed to offer a small smile to one of the puce-wearing bridesmaids as she tucked the list in her bag.

That tentative, rankleless smile died instantly as she spotted her mom entering the room. Morgan hurried toward her. "Annabelle?"

"Now, honey," her mother said quickly, her words tumbling over each other. "I didn't expect to see you here."

"I'm sure you didn't." Her mother couldn't help but hear the censure in her voice.

"But, sweetie, I'm not crashing. Scout's honor." She held up four fingers, which wasn't even close to the correct gesture, as she continued her hasty explanation. "There was a small accident and they needed another case of plates. It was on my way, so I just brought them myself."

Morgan noted her mother wasn't dressed in party clothes. Instead, she had on a long, buttoned trench coat, with trousers and black polished boots peeking out at the bottom.

"Where are you on your way to?" Morgan asked.

"Oh, just a little to-do."

"What kind of little to-do? Where are you going tonight, Mom?"

Conner came up behind her. "Why, Mrs. Miller, how nice to see you again."

"Conner, it's lovely seeing you as well. And now that I've delivered the plates, I have to run. Have a great time, you two. Don't do anything I wouldn't do." She looked at Conner and added, "That leaves you a lot of leeway, son." With a wink and a small wave, she hurried out.

Morgan wanted to melt into the floor, and was about to apologize when Conner started to laugh. "She's a riot."

"I don't know about that. She's more apt to *cause* a riot."

"You're her daughter. Children are supposed to be embarrassed by their parents."

"What about yours?" she asked. "You've never mentioned them."

He grew serious then, maybe a bit wistful. "They're both gone now. Your mother reminds me of my father. He was larger than life, always laughing. He thought of each day as a big adventure. My mother was quieter, but she always had a smile. They used to joke that Dad took her flying and she grounded him. They were that different, but they complemented each other. He was a salesman, she was a college professor. They came from very different backgrounds, but sort of balanced each other."

He gave his head a small shake. "Enough of that. I've got to get back to work."

"What do you need me to help with?"

"It's a smaller wedding, so there's not nearly as much to do. Take some time and work on your list. I've seen you scribbling."

"Thanks."

She found a quiet corner and worked for quite a while, until suddenly a light flashed in front of her. She looked up and there was another flash.

"Hey," she protested. "I hate having my picture taken."

"Just needed to finish off this roll before we left."

"We're done already?" she asked. "I got so busy with my list that I wasn't much help."

"No problem. We'll be ready to go in a few minutes."

The bride came over and started talking to Conner. Morgan waited patiently, considering the invitation she was sure would come. And with an almost forgotten sense of decisiveness, she knew she'd say yes.

Decision made, she even managed a smile for the sadistic bride as she left.

"So, are you ready?" Conner asked. "I'll drop you off at home."

Oh, he was going to be subtle. They'd pull up in front of her house and he'd say, in his most manly voice, *So, how do you feel about mind-blowing sex?*

She had her answer already.

THREE HOURS LATER, MORGAN WASN'T just in a funky mood, it had sunk lower to a dark one. And any mood lower than funky required an everything-but-the-kitchen-sink sundae to get her out of it. She'd picked up the supplies after Conner dropped her off with no mention of sex, mind-blowing or otherwise. Just a chaste kiss and a brief good-night.

To be fair, he'd been excited about a phone call from a friend urging him to get his résumé and portfolio together and send it out first thing Monday morning.

"I really do understand," she told Gilligan, who watched her assemble the sundae with interest gleaming in his eyes. "But he didn't even get out to walk me to the door. He was probably afraid I'd pull him in and make him have sex with me, and we wouldn't want that, would we?"

She topped off the marshmallow, M&Ms, chocolate sauce and strawberry ice cream mound with half a container of whipping cream.

Then she sat down on the stool and took a bite.

Annabelle burst in the back door without knocking. She eyed the bowl of ice cream, then studied Morgan with an uncharacteristic intensity. "Man troubles?"

Morgan didn't answer. She just took another bite.

"Well, I have a little problem I had hoped my daughter would help me with. And since she's home on a Friday night eating ice cream with the dog, she's obviously free to assist me."

"What now? And where were you going tonight?"

"I'll preface by saying that I didn't do anything illegal. I didn't even technically crash."

"Another reception?"

Annabelle snorted. "No. Of course not. There was a dearth of unattached men my age at receptions, remember?"

"Dearth?"

"Look it up."

"I know what it means, but it's not a word you normally use…." Morgan stopped. "You're trying to get me off track. What happened?"

"I went to the science fiction convention that's in town." She opened her trench coat to reveal a spandex jumpsuit. "First Lieutenant Annabelle Miller for the star ship *Expatriate*. You see, I was recruited. There are weekly meetings and I'm in charge of refreshments this week. I don't know how to get out of it. Not one of those boys is older than thirty. I'm many things, but I'm not a cradle robber."

Morgan wanted to be stern. Truly. But she couldn't quite manage it. She laughed. "Oh, Mom. Only you."

"Well, not necessarily only me. That's what I wanted to talk to you about. You see, my ensign, Charlie, is single and I thought that maybe you might like to come to our Monday night meeting. I know they'd be thrilled to have you visit. Maybe even join the crew."

Morgan had always liked science fiction shows, but she'd never felt the slightest urge to join an imaginary crew. And she definitely didn't want a uniform. "I don't think so."

"Oh, come on, don't be such a fuddy-duddy. Charlie and I are fixing each other up. He's bringing his dad and I'm bringing—"

"Someone other than me." Morgan switched tracks. "I mean, it wouldn't do to go out with Charlie and discover we might be able to have a relationship. It wouldn't be fair to either of us. I'm going home soon, remember?"

"Honey, sooner or later you're going to have to admit you are home."

With that, First Lieutenant Annabelle Miller flounced out Morgan's kitchen door and toward her own house.

Morgan didn't call out after her and explain things, for she suddenly wasn't sure she understood them herself. When she'd mentioned going home to San Diego, there wasn't that normal spurt of excitement.

As a matter of fact, she'd felt something more akin to…reluctance?

No, she wasn't going to explain anything to Annabelle until she figured a thing or two out for herself.

CHAPTER EIGHTEEN

Dear E.J., I've always thought of myself as decisive, but since coming home I feel lost. I don't know where to turn. Mom asked me if I wanted something because I wanted it, or because I thought I wanted it. Can you get so tied up in a goal, so used to viewing the world in such a narrow way, that you miss the bigger picture? Miss the fact you've changed, and that what you want has changed? I don't know.

BRIGHT AND EARLY SATURDAY MORNING, Morgan headed to Mark's office. It was an impressive high-rise, all metal and glass. She had a sugar hangover from last night's impressive sundae, and felt very little enthusiasm for this morning's meeting.

Mark himself came down to the lobby to escort her up to the fifteenth story, which housed Jameson, Inc.

The outer office spoke of refinement, of money, and beyond the door to the right of the receptionist's desk was a maze of cubicles. Even deserted, the area had a lot of energy. She could imagine the level of activity, the hum of voices, that would fill the huge space on weekdays. Real offices, with doors and windows, lined the outer edges of the floor.

"This is absolutely beautiful," Morgan declared as he settled her on the couch in his office.

She'd known that Mark was successful. She'd studied his business figures and realized that he had a Midas touch. Whatever new project he took on was bound to succeed. But knowing that, she still hadn't been prepared for the sleek, sophisticated, understated office.

This room was personal. One wall was filled with photos and awards, and his college diploma hung next to that from his grad school. A plaque honoring B. Mark Jameson for his continued support of his local alma mater was near a picture of him playing rugby.

"So, you did sports?" she said. Despite their lunch and dinner together, she didn't feel as if she knew much about him, other than business.

She realized she knew a lot more about Conner. His passion for his work. His care for his brother. Conner made her laugh and awoke feelings in her in a way that Mark never had.

As if to prove the point, Mark sat next to her and rested his hand against hers.

She waited, actively searching for a spark of something. There it was.

A niggle in the pit of her stomach. A warm, glowing feeling.

Well, maybe more of a hot feeling.

A burning feeling.

She realized that what she felt was an acid stomach, probably related to last night's sugarfest.

"I played rugby all four years of college...."

Nothing. She could sense no other hot-and-bothered feeling except the one in her stomach. And that didn't require anything more than a good antacid.

"...and my office..."

Why on earth didn't this perfect man, the type she'd always dreamed about, raise even the slightest spark?

"...I'd love to take you on a tour. I thought that I'd hire the same decorator to give OCDR a makeover when I buy it."

"If my mother decides to sell."

He nodded agreeably.

"Thanks for the tour offer, but I'd rather get down to business if you don't mind."

"If I do mind?"

Morgan hadn't known she'd made a decision until she heard herself say, "Mark, I think it would be better if we kept things between us on a professional level. I mean, you're a nice man, but I'm in town for only a little longer, and I think it would be wise if we both remember that."

She smiled, hoping to soften the fact she had rejected the idea of them dating. "I hope this won't affect our working together."

"I'm sorry you feel that way."

She watched him transform from hand-holding suitor to businessman in a heartbeat. "Of course, I'm still interested in buying the store."

"I'm glad." She pushed a sheet of paper toward him.

"Here are some of my mother's concerns. She'd want to be sure that she and Sunny both have a job, that…"

Item by item, she voiced her mother's concerns and terms, then they both bounced questions and answers back and forth.

An hour and a half later, Morgan gathered up her things. "Thank you, Mark. I think I have enough information to give my mother a realistic recommendation."

"Do you want to give me a hint what you'll be saying?"

"Not right now, but I'm sure Mom will be in touch soon."

"Morgan, about my job offer. I just want you to know that it isn't contingent on the other, more personal one. I have an eye for talent. I knew you had it when we met the first time, and after looking at your résumé, well, I want you. One way or another."

"Mark, I'm determined to go back to San Diego. I leave in just a couple of days for face-to-face interviews, although I've already spoken to both companies and feel pretty positive about my chances. As for something more than just business between us, you're a nice man. And under other circumstances, I'd have to be crazy not to explore a more personal relationship with you. But given the fact I'm leaving soon, well, I just want to say, I'm flattered. Thank you for the compliment."

She thought about extending her hand, but instead closed the distance between them and kissed his cheek.

Again, nothing happened. Not that she was surprised.

"Goodbye, Mark." She walked to the elevator and pressed the button for the lobby.

She'd made the right decision.

Okay, one decision down, countless left to go.

CHAPTER NINETEEN

E.J., sometimes all the apologizing in the world can't fix something's that's broken. And sometimes just a simple I'm sorry can fix a lot....

MORGAN STOOD OUTSIDE THE diner and realized she felt no pain. There was a sour sort of feeling churning in the pit of her stomach, though.

She'd had the same feeling the day she'd moved into the dorm, even though she'd known she was going to be rooming with Gina. College had been new, uncharted territory. There'd been no way to study, to prepare for what it would be like not to live at home.

She'd felt nauseous right up until the moment Gina had walked into their shared room and said, "This is going to be great."

And it had been. Gina, Sunny, Tessa, Nikki and

Morgan. Their five names had been forever linked on campus.

Then Morgan had left town. And the other four had gone on with the Sunday morning brunches without her.

It was time to put the group back together.

She took a deep breath, walked through the door and made her way back to the table…their table.

Four faces looked up at her. And the acid churning in her stomach felt as if it were burning a hole through the lining.

Then Gina smiled.

It wasn't the same unbridled smile of all those years ago. It was more cautious, but at the same time, hopeful.

"So, what'd I miss?" Morgan asked, as she took her seat.

"Gina was just telling us about the baby."

Gina looked at Morgan, obviously unsure if she should continue the story.

Morgan tried to offer an encouraging smile. "And?"

At that moment, it was as if they both knew some bridge existed where there hadn't been one before that morning. Their relationship wasn't what it once was, but they'd both left it room to grow into something more than it was right now.

Gina finished her story, and Morgan tried to throw out as casually as possible, "I've got tickets to San Diego for Tuesday."

Nikki sat up and peered out from beneath her sunglasses. "A job interview?"

"Two, as a matter of fact."

"Good for you," Sunny said, but her tone didn't match her words.

"I almost hate to go. I love this—being back with you, with *all* of you—again on Sundays." She looked directly at Gina as she said the words, and saw that her old friend knew what she meant.

"So why go?" Tess asked. "I'm sure there are jobs in Pittsburgh."

"As a matter of fact, I know there are. I've had an offer. A generous offer. But I don't live here anymore. I'm just visiting."

"Correct me if I'm wrong, but don't you own a house now?" Tessa, the lawyer, countered.

"A house I'm going to sell."

"And there are challenging jobs here…." Tessa pressed.

"Friends here," Nikki added.

"Family," Sunny said.

"There's us," Gina stated quietly. "Can San Diego offer as much?"

"I have a life there," Morgan protested. "I mean, I love that you all would like me to stay, but San Diego's home. And there's E.J. You'd all love him. He's a doctor. Right now he's in South America."

Sunny sighed, but picked up on Morgan's need to change the subject. "So how did you meet this E.J.?"

Morgan went into a monologue about that first meeting with E.J., in the emergency room, and then their Sunday mornings on the beach. She loved those mornings, but realized she loved this morning, as well.

She'd missed Sunday brunches before, but she'd been so busy being hurt that the missing was a side note. This time, it would be front and center.

She thought about her flight to San Diego on

Tuesday, waiting for the excitement to hit her. Maybe it was just too early, because she couldn't muster much.

Wanting to keep the conversation going in any direction but her move, she said, "I kissed two men this week."

Conversation came to an abrupt halt.

"And?" Sunny asked.

"So, how were they?" Nikki was once again peering at her with interest.

"One was bland at best. Decidedly so-so in my experience."

"Mark?" Sunny guessed.

Morgan nodded.

"And Conner kissed you as well?"

"Each time, it gets a little hotter. And I don't know why. He's not my type. I swear his entire wardrobe consists of denim and T-shirts. And shaving? Well, it's a when-the-stubble-itches-too-much-to-be-ignored sort of thing. He takes pictures for a living and doesn't work for a Fortune 500 company…."

"But?" Gina prompted.

"But." Morgan sighed. "But there's so much more to him than you'd expect. He gave up his dream job to be there for his brother. He seems to genuinely like my mother. And…I don't know. Being with him…"

"Zing," Gina whispered.

"Yeah. Zing. I don't seem to be able to control it."

"I don't think you can," Gina said. "It's either there or it's not."

Morgan didn't need to be overly insightful to realize they were no longer talking about herself and Conner.

Gina continued, "Sometimes when it's just there it's

so big it's palpable. You can try to fight against it, try to wish it away, but in the end, that kind of zing…"

Morgan knew Gina was referring to herself and Thomas. "Yes, zing. Sometimes, even if you want to, you can't ignore it."

"So what are you going to do?" Tessa asked.

"If we ever get our timing down, I think I'd like to explore our zing. I'm heading back to California, and he's got a hot lead on a new job. I guess I'll take interviews in San Diego and put my life back together."

"A life that doesn't include us," Sunny said sadly.

"Hey, does anyone want to know who I kissed this week after I got Morgan busted?" Nikki asked.

Morgan recognized that drawing the attention away from her was Nikki's intent. She shot her friend a smile of thanks.

The rest of the brunch was almost like old times. Almost. But as they finished and everyone started digging through wallets for plastic or cash to pay their checks, Morgan glanced at Gina, who flashed her a smile.

It would take time to rebuild their friendship, but Morgan was looking forward to it. To catching up, to rediscovering an old friend and maybe finding a new level to that friendship.

"You look happy," Sunny said softly.

"I am."

And as she said the words, she realized she was. Happy. Not in that big, ready to explode with it sort of way. But in a quieter, contented sort of way.

"Thank you," Gina said as they all walked to the cash register. "Thank you for giving me another chance."

Morgan couldn't think of any response to that. *You're*

welcome didn't sound quite right. She thought of saying, *I've missed you, too, only I didn't know it until I came home,* but she wasn't ready to voice those words yet. Maybe in time.

Rebuilding something with Gina *would* take time. But the fact was, Morgan didn't have much time left. She had interviews in San Diego, and once she got a new job, she'd be back out West for good. There was so much to do before that.

There was Conner. Her initial desire had only grown. She wanted him.

And the business. She wanted to see it settled for her mom, one way or the other.

Gina and her other friends. Morgan wanted more time with them as well.

"See you next week?" Tessa asked.

"Yes," she replied. She could promise that much. But after that, she hoped to be back in San Diego. She looked at Gina. "You?"

"I wouldn't miss it."

They all broke apart and went their separate ways. Morgan started the long walk home.

Time.

Suddenly it didn't seem as if she had enough.

CHAPTER TWENTY

Time. E.J., When I first got back to Pittsburgh, all I did was wonder how long it would be until I could come home to San Diego. But suddenly, it feels that when I do come back, I'll be leaving Pittsburgh too soon. There's just not enough time to do all the things I want to do....

ON MONDAY, AFTER PUTTING IN a full day at the OCDR office, Morgan finished packing her bag for her early flight the next day. She wasn't the least bit nervous about the interviews, which was odd, since her future relied on the impression she made at them.

She tried to weigh her emotions and realized she was pretty ambivalent about the entire trip.

"There's no sense of excitement," she told Gilligan,

who was watching her pack with all the interest of someone watching paint dry.

"Yoo-hoo," she heard her mother holler from the kitchen.

"There's your pet-sitter," Morgan told the old dog, who took off at a good clip for someone as geriatric as he was.

"Hi, Mom," Morgan said, following him into the kitchen. "Gilligan's easy to find, but I don't have a clue how we're going to get the cats to come out. I've only caught the barest glimpses of them on occasion. I don't think they like me."

Annabelle laughed. "Of course they like you. They're just shy. When Auggie bought them, Gilligan here was in his prime, and what with his little humping problem, they learned early on that being invisible was safer. I guess now that Gilligan's too old to do more than think about his favorite pastime, their habits are too well set to change. But watch." She picked up the box of food Morgan had set out on the table, and shook it.

The two cats didn't quite burst into the room; that would be too far beneath their dignity. But they did waltz out of whatever shadows they'd been lurking in, and gave Annabelle and Morgan a this-had-better-be-good look of disdain.

Annabelle sprinkled a bit of the kibble in the cage and Thurston and Lovey walked right in.

"It's a matter of knowing how to attract them. In this case, kibble. So, you're leaving early tomorrow morning?"

"Very early. So we'll say our goodbyes now."

"I'll miss you." Her mother looked dejected, an expression she rarely wore. Her perpetual good spirits always buoyed Morgan. Oh, Annabelle could and did make her crazy, but she also always made her feel… safe. Better. Happy.

She gave her mom a quick hug. "Hey, it's only a couple days."

Annabelle hugged her back, maybe a little too hard, a little too long. "But this is the beginning of the end. One of these companies will be sure to snap you up, and you'll move back across the country again."

"Well, we'll still have some time. I have to clean out the house and make arrangements for it. I found an auction service that will come in, give me a flat rate for everything in here, but I need to go through all Uncle Auggie's personal things and decide what to keep, what to let go. And I have to finalize my report for you."

"Report? You can't just tell me what you think?"

She shook her head. "Mom, what I think doesn't matter. This decision is all about you…about what's going to make you happy. Do you want to run the store as is? Expand it? Do you want to sell to Mark? His offer seems solid, although I still feel as if I'm missing something. We'll have Tessa check over the fine points on the contract if that's the way you decide to go. I've prepared a chart for you with the pros and cons of each of those options. You'll have to decide which one is going to make you happy."

"That's all I want for *you,* Morgan. I want you to be happy. Are you sure California is the place for that? It seems to me you've been pretty happy since you got home. Watching you at the office, working away, reconnecting with your friends…you look happy."

"I am. I've enjoyed visiting home. But then, I'd love visiting Paris, or London, or Disney World. Any of them, all of them, would make me happy. But my home is in San Diego. I'm thrilled to be going back."

But even as she said it, she realized that wasn't quite true. *Ambivalent* didn't equal *thrilled*.

"Well, then, that's that," Annabelle said with a watery smile. "I won't try to fix you up anymore. I found Charlie another girl."

"So, you're still serving as lieutenant on the ship?"

"It was first lieutenant," Annabelle corrected. "And no, I'm not serving. I resigned my commission. I had my eye on Charlie's dad, but it didn't work out. I need a man who thinks I hung the moon, not one who wants to pretend to orbit the moon with me."

"I'm sorry, Mom."

Annabelle shook off her momentary frustration and resumed her normally positive expression. "Now, don't worry. I'll find my man eventually."

"I know you will." Morgan knew that in addition to being one of the most upbeat people in the world, her mom was also one of the most single-minded. She was going to find her man, of that Morgan was sure. But she was hit with a wave of regret that she wouldn't be here to witness it when it happened. "You'll have to call and keep me posted."

"I will, but even though we call, it's not the same."

"No, it's not the same. But it's the next best thing. And hey, if you sell the company, you'll have time to come out to California and visit. A nice, long visit. Maybe your Mr. Right is waiting for you there."

Annabelle shrugged. "We'll see. But truth be told, I doubt he is. My home is here in Pittsburgh. I'm sure I'll find him here. I just have to keep looking."

"God help Pittsburgh," Morgan muttered to herself as Annabelle took the cat carrier and Gilligan's leash and left.

So, now what?

The house was empty. No Gilligan, no lurking cats. Morgan's suitcase was packed, and she filled a few of her empty minutes by taking it out to the car and locking it in the truck. She checked that her wallet was in her purse and her ID in her wallet. She had her airline confirmation numbers and…

The night sort of stretched out ahead of her.

She should have asked her mother if she wanted to do pizza and a movie. She still could call.

The phone rang.

Kismet, she thought as she answered, "Hello?"

CONNER STARED AROUND THE apartment. It seemed… empty.

They'd moved Ian over to his new place earlier. Sunny and Johnny had come to help him settle in. Not that Johnny was a great help, but the baby seemed to enjoy shredding the newspaper packing, and kept them all amused.

Ian had invited Conner to stay for dinner, but he could sense his brother and Sunny were looking forward to some time alone, so he'd bowed out…and come home to this very empty apartment.

But, to be honest, it wasn't the emptiness of the apartment that had him calling Morgan. It was need, pure and simple.

After the wedding, he'd planned on inviting her over, but Luke's call had him scrambling to put a portfolio of his work together. It had taken all night. He'd agonized over each picture.

He'd put the samples of his work, along with a résumé, in the mail today. He'd done all he could.

And he found he needed to see Morgan.

Needed to touch her.

Needed some time alone with her. Time without her friends, without his brother and without her mother.

Morgan was leaving for San Diego the next day, but for tonight, he wanted her all to himself.

No strings to get entangled in.

It was a perfect situation.

Which was why he was puzzled as to why it didn't feel so perfect.

He saw her car pull up in front of the house and hurried to open the door before she had a chance to knock.

She held a pizza box in one hand, a bottle of wine in the other. "I brought dinner."

He ushered her in and found himself grinning, though he wasn't sure why. Maybe it was just the simple fact that he was glad to see her. "Looks good. And I'm not talking about the pizza or the wine."

She blushed. "I hope you're hungry."

"Oh, I am," he assured her as he shut the door and moved closer. She looked a bit hesitant, so he stepped back again. "You seem nervous."

"I am."

He took another step back, thinking he must have misread where their relationship was going.

"Then let's eat," he said, hoping to put her at ease. He started toward the kitchen, but noticed she wasn't following.

He turned. "Morgan?"

"Truth is, I don't want pizza or wine. I want…" She

let the sentence trail off, but he could see that he hadn't misread anything, because what she wanted was there in her eyes.

"Me, too," he agreed.

ME, TOO.

Morgan almost sighed with relief when she heard Conner utter those words. She knew there was an attraction between them, knew he wanted her, but after the chaste kiss following the last wedding she'd felt unsure.

Me, too. That was all the reassurance she needed. She tossed the pizza onto the hallway table, set the wine next to it and launched herself into Conner's open arms.

She didn't feel the least bit shy, which was funny, because being this bold with a man she'd known such a limited amount of time wasn't the least bit like her.

She wrapped her arms around him and kissed him with all the pent-up longing and desire she'd been holding back. She kissed him until she practically forgot to breathe.

"Your room?" she asked.

"You're sure?" he countered.

"Yes." Their sentences were short and concise, as if there was too much going on in their heads to spare much thought for putting words together. And, after all, she didn't really think many words were needed.

He led her to his room, holding her hand, as if losing physical contact would hurt.

Morgan had never been a fan of sex with a new partner. Not that she'd had all that many first times, but it always felt awkward. The what-ifs tended to intrude, and they did now.

She unbuttoned her blouse. What if Conner preferred big-busted women? What if he noticed that extra ten pounds she'd been meaning to lose? What if the scar from her appendectomy was a turnoff? What if—

"You're beautiful," he murmured, helping her slip the blouse from her shoulders, then running a fingertip from her neck down her arm, a light caress.

The what-ifs didn't exactly disappear, but they faded as he looked at her with unabashed appreciation in his eyes.

Feeling bold, she untucked his T-shirt from his jeans and slowly pulled it up, then off. His chest was broad and well toned. She splayed her hand against it, loving the soft hair contrasting with the hard muscles.

He pulled her close and kissed her again, and she loved how they fit together so perfectly. She tucked nicely into his embrace, just tall enough to reach his lips without straining.

Lips to lips, chest to chest, they explored each other, claimed each other.

When they finally broke apart, she realized he'd removed her bra. "Cool trick," she teased as he dangled it from his finger.

"I have other tricks. Wanna see?" He wiggled his eyebrows suggestively and she chuckled.

Laughing while making love…she'd never had that kind of relationship with anyone before. But with Conner it felt right. She unbuttoned her slacks and let them slide to the floor.

He followed suit.

She took a step toward him, but he stopped her. "Wait a moment." He studied her, as if committing every inch of her body to memory. His look of appreciation, paired with his obvious desire, kept her from feeling awkward. Instead she felt desirable. She knew he wasn't noticing her flaws.

"Beautiful," he said again, then opened his arms.

Kissing Conner, being lowered to the bed, exploring every inch…it didn't feel like an introduction. It felt like coming home.

When he opened the nightstand drawer and took out a foil packet, rather than breaking the cadence of their foreplay, it became a part of it. Slowly, gently, she slid the condom home. His body arched, telling her without words he couldn't take much more teasing. Telling her again moments later, as he entered her, how much he'd wanted this. They found their rhythm, slow and easy. It gradually built in speed and intensity.

Conner held himself back. He'd never felt this much for any woman, never wanted so badly to drive into her and find his own release. But he held on, letting the tempo carry Morgan, pushing her to the brink. Her eyes were closed, but he kept his open, watching her as her body tensed, seeing the moment when she went over the edge. As she gasped, he finally let himself go, faster, harder, driving home. Joining her in release.

He collapsed on top of her, still needing her touch, not wanting to let her go.

His mind was hazy and the only coherent thought he could seem to manage was, *this*.

This. He felt as if he'd waited for this forever, even though he knew it hadn't been long.

"Conner, I can't breathe," Morgan said a hint of laughter as she gave him a slight push.

He obliged, rolling to the side, but pulled her with him so they were face-to-face, the contact unbroken.

"That was…" He paused, not able to find the proper words.

"Yes, it was," she said.

Morgan snuggled close. Even after their amazing time together, she still craved his touch.

He brushed a stray wisp of hair off her face. "I want a picture of you looking like this."

"Like what?"

"Content. Beautiful."

"Well satisfied," she added, smiling. "Very, very well satisfied."

He chuckled. "Why, thank you, ma'am."

It felt so right, to be here in Conner's arms, teasing, touching. As if there were no one in the world but them, and time had stopped.

But her bubble of happiness burst as a sad fact crept in. Morgan knew that her all-the-time-in-the-world feeling was an illusion. They didn't have it and she was hit by a stab of regret. She was sorry her hours with this amazing man, amazing lover, would be so short.

She was determined to enjoy every minute she did have with him.

"Do you have to go home tonight because of the dog?" Conner whispered in her ear.

"No. Mom took the pets tonight because my flight's so early in the morning. I'm all packed and my luggage is in the car."

"Good. Good that she's got your pets, not good about the flight," he clarified. "Will you spend the night? My place is closer to the airport than yours."

She paused, then asked as she smiled, "If I say yes, can we have a repeat performance?"

"I think that could be arranged." His stomach growled. "But first, how do you feel about eating cold pizza while you're naked in bed?"

"Is there any other way to eat it?" she asked, and laughed for no reason other than she was here in Conner's bed and couldn't remember the last time she'd felt so happy. Felt a warm glow that seemed to envelope her completely.

It wasn't that they'd made love, though that had been fantastic.

It wasn't the idea of eating pizza naked in bed with him.

It was just Conner.

He was here; so was she.

That's all it took.

She was simply happy and she refused to analyze it any more than that.

MORGAN WOKE UP ON HER side in Conner's bed. He was nestled against her, his arm draped over her stomach. A hint of sunlight peeked beneath the window's blind, and someone close by was running a lawnmower. It wasn't so near that the noise was offensive, just a mild little hum.

She smiled. This was the perfect way to wake up.

She glanced at the clock and her smile faded.

It was 8:03.

She should be sitting at the airport right now, waiting to board her plane. A plane that was due to take off at 8:46.

The airport was at least…what? Half an hour away, maybe quite a bit more with traffic?

She'd never make it there, much less through check-in and security, on time.

She was screwed.

She had appointments. And even if she could get a later flight out, she'd never get there in time for her interviews.

She waited for the sinking feeling in the pit of her stomach—waited for that spurt of panic to send adrenaline rushing through her system.

Waited for something.

And as she tried to analyze her feelings, she found there was one predominant one in the forefront: relief.

It didn't make sense. She wanted to go back to her life in San Diego, didn't she?

Conner stirred, not waking up, but reaching for her in his sleep and pulling her closer. She went obligingly.

Was he the reason for this hesitation about leaving?

That didn't make sense, either. This was casual. He was leaving Pittsburgh as well, to chase after his dream job in some big city.

Slowly, she eased out of bed, trying not to wake him, retrieved a flannel shirt from the back of his chair and tiptoed out of the room.

She found her purse in the living room and called both companies, knowing it was far too early in California for anyone to be in, but wanting to leave a message on their answering machines. She promised both to call later in the day and reschedule if they were still interested in interviewing her. Then she phoned the airline to see about arranging another flight out.

That done, she went toward the kitchen to start some coffee, but on her way down the hall, she passed the door that Conner had told her led to his darkroom. She opened it and felt for a switch.

As she turned it on, she blinked and waited for her eyes to adjust. There was traditional developing equipment and a computer and a huge tank of a printer, probably for his digital shots.

She turned toward the other wall and sucked in her breath at what she saw. It was covered with a dizzying array of photos.

Nature shots mixed with wedding photos. Trees. Frogs. A pond. Brides. Grooms. Then she spotted a number of herself. That first reception she'd crashed, when he'd claimed he'd been testing his flash. Wearing that hideous pink monstrosity of a bridesmaid dress. Her standing with the puce bride. Candid shots she'd been unaware of.

Morgan had never considered herself photogenic. She had a habit of squinting, or grimacing at the precise moment the camera clicked. But these were as good as she'd ever looked on film.

Smiling. Laughing. Appearing intent, or lost in thought. Looking at them made her feel exposed. As if Conner saw things she almost wished he didn't.

She decided it was sort of narcissistic, studying herself in that way, so she concentrated on the other pictures.

She moved farther down the wall, and studied more of the nature shots. The frog with its tongue extended, presumably to catch its lunch. A fox peeking through underbrush. A field filled with deer grazing, one lone doe with her head up, cocked to one side as if she heard something. Morgan had thought she knew a fair bit about Conner. She'd discovered his sense of humor, his loyalty and caring for his brother. But here, in these pictures, she learned even more. He was an artist. He saw the world with an artist's eye.

"So, what do you think?"

She jumped and turned. She knew she was grinning like a moonstruck teenager, but she couldn't help it. He was amazing. She wondered how she'd ever lucked into finding him.

Her mom.

Morgan was eventually going to have to thank Annabelle for getting her to that wedding so they could meet.

"What do you think?" he repeated.

Before she could tell him how wonderful she thought he was, and gush all over him, he added, "About the pictures?"

"Oh, the pictures? They're amazing, really art. You're a brilliant photographer."

She kissed his cheek in greeting. "You've got an incredible talent. Conner, you've captured life there. Milestones in people's lives, and precious moments in nature. On one level you preserve history, record a special event, and on another, you create art."

He shrugged, as if he didn't quite know how to cope with her compliments.

She let him off the hook and changed the subject. "I was on my way to make coffee. You interested?"

"First I wanted to find you and do this…." He kissed her. It was a friendly, good-morning sort of kiss. "Then I was after some coffee myself."

She burrowed her face in his chest and inhaled.

He laughed. "What was that all about?"

She could feel her cheeks warm as she admitted,

"That first night we met? I thought you were cute. But right after that, I caught a whiff of you, and my second thought was that you smelled good. You still do."

"Glad I showered before you checked," he said with a laugh. Then he leaned over and made a great show of sniffing her back. "Let me return the compliment."

"I haven't showered yet."

"Doesn't matter. You still smell good." He took her hand and started out of the room.

"I missed my flight," she blurted.

He dropped her hand and turned toward her, his response right there in his expression. "Oh, shit, Morgan, here we were, playing some kind of scratch-and-sniff game, and I totally forgot about your going to San Diego this morning. Shit," he repeated.

"It's all right."

"No, it's not. I'm so sorry. We should have set the alarm. Did you call and see if there was a later flight? I could drive you to the airport." Conner seemed so much more upset than she felt.

She tried to ease his obvious distress. "Hey, don't worry. I called and left a message at both places. I'll re-schedule if they're still interested in meeting with me."

He didn't look the least bit calmer. "But—"

She gently put a finger to his lips to silence him. "No buts about it. It's fine."

"But what if you lose the positions to someone else?"

It was her turn to shrug. "Then they weren't the jobs I was meant to have."

"Morgan."

"Conner," she said, mimicking his exasperated inflection. "Don't go messing with my view of destiny. I'll get the job I was meant to get. I've worked too hard for too long not to. But maybe destiny had something other than interviews planned for me today."

"Like what?"

"Your brother's moved out, and my mother is pet sitting. No one expects to see me in Pittsburgh today at all. Oh, what do you think we should do with our time?"

She winked and tried to assume what she hoped was a seductress's expression. "And let me assure you the only answer I'm looking for involves you, me and your bedroom."

His tense expression finally relaxed. "I hadn't thought about that particular fringe benefit. May I say, I like how your mind works, Morgan Miller?"

"And I like how your—" she whispered the word "—works."

He laughed. "Let's get that coffee, then go see how well it's working this morning."

THEY STAYED IN BED FOR THE greater part of the morning, but they spent more time talking than having sex.

"I want to capture big events on film," he told her.

"And you had that kind of job offer before your brother got injured. You gave up that dream in order to take care of him. That says something about you, Conner Danning."

She mussed his hair, mainly just for an excuse to touch him.

Touching him. It was an addiction. She couldn't get enough.

"Taking care of each other, that's what family does."

"Not all families, but the good ones. And you're a good one."

Again he looked embarrassed by her praise, so he just shrugged it off. "I didn't really give it up, I just delayed it."

"So you're leaving, just like you planned."

"Just like I planned. I sent out my résumé and portfolio yesterday. I'll be starting at the bottom, but I'll be starting. I hope to be in D.C. in a few weeks."

"You must be thrilled."

"Yeah, I must be." Funny thing was he didn't sound particularly thrilled. "And speaking of thrilled…I can think of something I'd find even more thrilling…."

He leered at her, but unfortunately, his smile ruined the effect.

Sometime after lunch she called the two businesses in San Diego. The time difference made it still early in the morning there.

Conner hovered behind her, looking worried.

She hung up the phone and offered him a reassuring smile. "I leave tomorrow morning, same time I was supposed to go this morning. They were very nice about it. But let's not test the scope of their forgiveness. We'll set the alarm this time. Let's do it right now, as a matter of fact."

"I think that would be wise."

She knew that when she left the next day, the magic would end. She'd be back on the road to California. Conner would be getting ready for his new job.

They'd both be leaving Pittsburgh.

Leaving each other.

And despite the fact she'd known him for only a short while, the thought hurt.

CHAPTER TWENTY-ONE

ANNABELLE LIKED TO BELIEVE SHE LIVED her life as if the glass was perpetually half-full. But today, her glass wasn't just half-empty, it was bone dry.

She'd had such high hopes for this new man. He'd seemed so nice, so normal. Since she was pet-sitting Gilligan, she'd decided to enroll him in obedience class. Of course, due to his age, the only command he really listened to was "down." He'd seemed quite content to sprawl on the floor and watch the rest of the dogs perform.

That was until Hershal walked in with Miss Muffy, a very refined toy poodle. Gilligan suddenly remembered there was more to life than napping, and tried to show his appreciation of Muffy's refined poodle beauty. Unfortunately, neither Muffy nor Hershal was impressed by his rediscovered humping abilities.

Annabelle had protested that Gilligan wasn't even

her dog, and that's when she was unceremoniously kicked out of the class. Ron and his boxer had followed them out. They'd gone for a coffee, and Annabelle had thought she'd found a man with potential.

Instead he was a jerk.

A real, honest-to-goodness cad. He'd led her on. And she'd never have known the truth if she hadn't called his office in the morning to tell him how much she'd enjoyed meeting him last night, only to have his secretary inform her that he'd been rushed to the hospital with an apparent heart attack.

Annabelle had hurried to his side, and found his wife already ensconced there.

His wife.

The two-timing, double-dipping, balding, slightly paunchy cad. Annabelle might have been inclined to go easy on him, but it turned out not to be a heart attack, just a bad case of gas, like Sunny's mother. Annabelle wondered how often gas attacks were mistaken for heart attacks.

It really didn't matter.

She'd met the wife, informed the poor woman what a scum-sucker she was married to, tossed a small yellow pitcher of water on the gassy two-timer and walked out of the emergency room.

She would have driven home, but was feeling too upset. Thankfully, she'd found this quiet meeting room. She had to get herself calmed down before she climbed behind the wheel.

She took a deep, cleansing breath.

She'd told Morgan she was lonely, but that description sounded too tame. She felt an aching hole in her life. She missed having a partner, and was beginning to think that she'd never find someone.

"That's it," she said aloud to the empty room. "I'm done. Quitting cold turkey."

Yes, no more crashing for Annabelle Miller. She'd rather spend the rest of her days alone than go through another humiliating experience like that.

"That's good," said a rich male voice from behind her. "Admitting you have a problem is the first step. Quitting cold turkey, a good second one."

Annabelle took in the lovely man standing in the doorway. Salt-and-pepper hair, thick glasses and a suit that looked as if it had just come out of some 1980s mothballs.

But then he smiled.

She forgot geek glasses and the bad suit as she smiled back.

"I'm Todd, by the way."

"I'm…" It took her a second to remember her name because he was still smiling and it was hard to think when faced with that.

"Annabelle," she finally managed to blurt, feeling breathless either from the effort of remembering her name, or because of Todd. She wasn't sure.

"I'm Annabelle," she repeated for good measure.

"Well, Annabelle, we're glad you're here. It takes a lot of courage to admit you have a problem with alcohol." He nodded at the small pin on his lapel. "Ten years for me. I wear this suit to meetings to remind myself of the decade plus I lost to alcohol. Then I found AA and… well, like I said, it's been ten years. This your first meeting?"

She nodded.

Meeting?

AA?

Alcohol.

Oh, no. Despite her resolution a few minutes ago, it would appear that she'd crashed an A.A. meeting. She should go. She should explain to Todd why she'd been in here.

"Want to help me set up?" he asked.

She smiled. "I would. I definitely would."

CHAPTER TWENTY-TWO

E.J., I'm leaving Pittsburgh and heading to San Diego for those interviews. I'll be staying at your apartment… thanks for the key. I'm not as excited as I thought I'd be. Maybe it's because I know you won't be there waiting for me, or maybe…

WEDNESDAY AFTERNOON, MORGAN BREATHED a sigh of relief. She was pretty sure that the interviews had gone well. Ellie Marx at Turner, Inc. had asked if she'd come back again the next day. Morgan was glad she'd booked a flight late tomorrow. She'd meet with Ms. Marx in the morning, then head back to Pittsburgh.

In the meantime, she had the rest of the day here in San Diego. She planned to reacquaint herself with the city, and in the process, she was bound to remember how much she loved it here and why.

She dropped her stuff off at E.J.'s, then headed to Manny's, her favorite restaurant. The food was great, but that wasn't what kept her coming back. Right after she'd moved to San Diego she'd discovered the midpriced restaurant and had fallen in love with the view.

She waited for the feeling of home to steal over her as she was led to a table on the dcck. It was three o'clock, an off hour, so she lucked into a seat at the railing. She inhaled deeply and took in the sounds of the waves slapping the rocky shore. A cool breeze blew in off the water and tickled her bare arms.

Normally, this was a moment when she'd feel that deep sense of peace and purpose steal over her. Today? She felt as restless as one of the waves, washing back and forth. Back and forth.

"Hey, you," a voice said from behind her.

Morgan didn't have to turn to know who it was. She jumped up and simply drank in the sight of E.J. He was maybe five-ten on a good shoe day, and his reddish-brown hair was sorely in need of a trim. Oh, who was she kidding? The man had enough hair for six people and it seemed bound and determined to behave as if it were on six different people's heads, part of it curling, another part cowlicky, some just standing straight on end for the sheer heck of it. But when it was added to his abundance of freckles and devilishly wicked grin, it worked. E.J. would never be the kind of man women drooled over, but he was cute and he was here.

She couldn't hold back any longer. She hugged him. "E.J., how did you find me? When did you get back? How are you?" Questions tumbled out, one after another.

Seeing E.J., Morgan finally achieved a bit of the sense of coming home she'd been waiting for.

"I just saw your suitcase in the living room so I knew you were back in town. As for how I found you, it wasn't rocket science. You love this place. To answer your second question, I got in yesterday. My replacement showed up early, so I jumped on a flight right away. I e-mailed and called you—"

"I wasn't at home."

"I got that. So I tried your cell."

"I turned it off last night." She hadn't wanted to pick up any messages from her mom because she didn't want to answer any sticky how-did-the-interviews-go question. "I meant to turn it on when I got off the plane today, but obviously forgot."

"So, if you weren't here last night and you weren't at your place…Conner's?" She must have looked surprised because E.J. said, "I read your e-mails last night while I tried to get hold of you. All your e-mails. Your many, very frequent, at least daily e-mails filled with all the tidbits from your visit in Pittsburgh."

"Sorry," Morgan said. "You weren't home and weren't answering and I guess…well, the e-mails were sort of like a diary. 'Dear E.J., my life's a mess.' It was cathartic and sort of anonymous. I could keep sending them out, but nothing was coming back. I just forgot that eventually you'd come home and have to sift through them all."

He laughed in that E.J., you're-so-funny sort of way. "No problem. I felt as if I was here for it all. I missed you."

"How was the trip?" she asked, hoping if he talked about the last few weeks away saving the world she wouldn't feel so selfishly focused on her own turmoil.

"It went well." He got a weird look on his face. Mysterious.

"What?" she demanded.

"I know you don't want to hear the intimate details of my surgeries—even thinking about blood makes you sick to your stomach. And having experienced that once first-hand, I prefer avoiding a repeat performance. But I do want to hear the details of what you've been up to in Pittsburgh. How's Annabelle? Still crashing? And this Conner, please tell me he's more of a man than Marvin ever was."

"Marvin was a putz," she admitted. "He called me there once, wanting to get back together, but having some distance between us helped me realize that no matter what, that wasn't going to happen. I should have listened to you a long time ago."

"Yes, you should have. But then, your stubbornness is one of the qualities I like about you...except when you're stubbornly refusing to listen to my very sage, big brotherish sort of advice. Then I hate it. But back to the question at hand. Tell me about Conner."

"That's not a question, it's a decree." He just sat there, waiting. Morgan gave in. "He's definitely not a putz, but not my type. To be honest, it doesn't really matter if he's my type or not because if these interviews went as well as I think they went, then I'll be in San Diego soon."

"You used to say 'home.' San Diego was home. But now?"

"Send a surgeon to South America to save a few lives and he comes back thinking he's Freud," she groused. "San Diego *is* home. I belong here. I've built a life here. I have plans, goals that all center on my being here."

"Plans change. Goals, too. I know about your lists, but all it takes to change things on that is crossing out one goal and writing in another. So, the question isn't what did you plan, it's what do you want. What *do* you want now? That's what you have to answer."

"Freud. You think you're freakin' Freud. A man with all the deep psychological answers."

"No. I think I'm your friend. And from what I read in all those e-mails, I think the time has come for you to reassess your goals and maybe set new ones. What do you want now, Morgan? What's going to make you happy?" He reached out and took her hand, patting it in that big brother way. "That's all I want for you."

"What do I want? What's going to make me happy? Damned if I know," she muttered.

"Don't you think you'd better find out?"

CHAPTER TWENTY-THREE

E.J., it's so good having you home again....

HOME.

That was Morgan's first thought as her plane set back down in Pittsburgh early Friday. She was exhausted after flying all night, but she was anxious to tell her mother and her friends about the interviews. She couldn't wait to pick up Gilligan and the cats.

And Conner? There were a whole host of things she couldn't wait to do with Conner. And it wasn't just what she wanted to do with him. She couldn't wait to tell him about the whole trip.

She'd thought about calling him half-a-dozen times while she waited for her plane. But it was too early and she wasn't sure they had that type of relationship.

Oh, she wouldn't hesitate with E.J., but she knew

exactly what their relationship was. Friends. Best friends. No hope of being anything more. Once a woman barfed on a man's shoes, she'd pretty much drawn a line in the sand that relationships were built on.

But Conner?

They'd slept together. They'd hung out. But their relationship couldn't go any further than casual.

The drive home from the airport seemed to take far longer than it should. She'd read somewhere that time wasn't stationary, that it expanded and contracted given the proper circumstances. So the fact that it was stretching, taking too long to get home couldn't possibly have anything to do with the turmoil her mind was in. It had to be some kind of time-warp thing.

Morgan turned the radio up as loud as it would go, hoping to drown out her way-too-active thoughts. But after about ten minutes she admitted that not only wasn't it drowning out her racing mind, it was giving her a headache, so she turned it back down.

When on earth had she become the kind of person who didn't listen to music blaringly loud?

Could it be that sometime when she wasn't looking she'd become a grown-up?

Not an enticing thought, because adults should have all the answers, and to be honest, though she didn't enjoy her music as loud as she used to, she wasn't sure she had any more answers than before.

She pulled into the drive at her house, and barely had the suitcase out of the backseat when her mother came out of her house holding Gilligan's leash and carrying the cat carrier.

She hurried over to Morgan. "So, how did it go?" Annabelle asked without preamble.

"Come on in and I'll tell you all about it."

Her mother followed her into the house and set the carrier down. "You're not looking as happy as I thought you would. But you don't look distraught, either." She unhooked Gilligan's lead.

Morgan set her suitcase down and watched as the dog walked around in a circle, sniffing the room, then collapsed in a heap.

"I'm happy," she said. "Of course I'm happy. It all went very well. I had a second interview with Turner, Inc., and they offered me the job."

"Oh. So, when are you leaving?" her mother asked, with what sounded like resignation in her voice.

"I didn't give them a definite answer. If I accept the position, I won't start for a few weeks. Enough time to get the house cleared out and on the market. If you're agreeable, I thought I'd have a power-of-attorney drawn up so that you could sign whatever papers need to be signed for both the real estate agent and the eventual closing."

"You don't want to come home for that?"

Morgan shook her head. "No, it's not that I don't want to come back. It's just that I don't know if I'll be able to. I'll be busy at a new job and there's just no way to know if I'd be able to get the time off."

Morgan knelt down next to the carrier and peeked in. "Hi, guys. I hope you'll come out a bit more often now." She unlocked the door. The two cats were out like a streak, and Morgan expected them to go back into whatever nether region of the house they liked to lurk in. But instead they went as far as the middle of the living room, where they found a patch of sunlight and sprawled in it, looking totally content to be home.

She stood and motioned for Annabelle to follow her into the kitchen. "Anyway, if you're able to take care of it, and willing, that's one less thing I'll have to worry about."

"You know I'll do it," her mother said. "But for the record, I don't like the thought of your leaving."

"I think I'd feel unloved if you were too overjoyed at the prospect of me going." Morgan was teasing, but it seemed to fall flat. "Anyway, thanks."

"Those animals are glad you're back," Annabelle said. "Have you thought about what you're going to do with them when you move back to California?"

"I figured if you didn't want them, I'd take them with me. I missed them."

"I guess it would be nice to have someone to come home to."

"I'll miss having you next door, popping in whenever." That surprised Morgan. She loved her mother, always had, always would, but living next to her? She hadn't anticipated enjoying it. But she did. She enjoyed working with her, as well. "Mom, about OCDR?"

"Your suggestions were wonderful, Morgan. But to be honest, I just don't want to expand. Mark's offer looks fair, and he'll promise to keep me and Sunny on the payroll. I think we could come to a deal. I was hoping you'd pin down the terms with him tonight. I've got a meeting set up."

"You know I will, if you're sure. Though, I think the expansion ideas would eventually make you a lot more money than selling will."

"But it would take a lot of time, I'm just not willing

to spend that much on something that would be work. I like coming in on time, then clocking out. I know that you think I should expand and I'm sorry that I can't."

Morgan thought about the store, about all the potential. She was sure it would be a real success, but she could also tell that her mother just didn't have the heart for it. "You have nothing to be sorry about, Mom."

"I can see how enthusiastic you were about the expansion ideas. It was there on every page. Your plans are wonderful and I do see the potential. That's why, before I make any final deal with Mark, I wanted to discuss one other option with you." She paused, looking uncharacteristically unsure. "I thought I'd offer the store to you."

"What?"

"I'd like to let you buy the store," Annabelle said with deliberate slowness. "You could stay here and set your expansion plans into motion. We'd work out a way for you to purchase the store in bits and pieces, out of the profits the expansion generates. It would be all legal. You'd own it, run it, and I could go back to doing what I love, just working nine to five and living my life without all the worries and responsibilities."

"Mom…" Morgan couldn't quite decide how to answer. "San Diego's my home."

"So's Pittsburgh. There's nothing saying you have to go back to California. You could stay here."

"This new job is everything I always dreamed of. A lot more responsibility than my old one and room to move up the corporate ladder. It's what I went to school for, what I've worked for. What I've always wanted."

"Sometimes what we think we want isn't what we want at all."

"But—"

Annabelle held up her hand, silencing Morgan. "Don't say no. Think about it. And remember, the direction you've always been headed in might not be the right one for you anymore. You'd be leaving a lot behind if you leave. Your friends. The memories. Me."

"Oh, Mom, I know, but—"

ANNABELLE INTERRUPTED AGAIN. She had things to say, and she was finally going to say them all. "Morgan, honey, when you left five years ago you were hurt, you were running away from the pain and trying to find out who you were. Well, you've managed that splendidly. You know who you are. Anyone who meets you can't help but see who you are—a strong, intelligent woman with a great capacity to love."

"Mom…" Morgan let that one word hang there a moment. "I truly don't know what to say."

Annabelle looked at her, and studying her the way mothers sometimes do. Her daughter was amazing.

How on earth she'd ever raised such a smart, independent, talented girl was truly a mystery. Annabelle knew she'd never been a traditional mother, but she loved the woman sitting across from her.

It's true, they might not always see eye to eye, but God, she loved her.

"Listen, you just talk to Mark, then decide what you want to do. Don't make a decision based on what you think you should do, what you think I want, or what anyone else wants. Ask yourself what *you* want and where you really belong. If the answer is California…well, I'll just have to get used to making more cross-country flights."

Morgan leaned over and hugged her. "I can't promise anything other than to think about it," she said. "But one way or another, thanks for the option."

"Hey, what's a mother for?" They broke apart. Annabelle patted at her eyes, hoping her makeup hadn't run. "Now, if you excuse me, I was just getting ready for a date when you pulled up."

"With who?"

"I don't want to jinx it, so I'm not saying."

"Mom," Morgan said, a warning note in her voice.

Annabelle had so much on her mind. Morgan. The store. And as much as they were both worries, her excitement about another date with Todd overruled everything.

"Fine. Don't jinx it. Go have fun."

Annabelle had confessed last night that she'd crashed—inadvertently crashed—the AA meeting.

She was done crashing. And all she could hope was that her daughter was finally willing to admit San Diego was a nice place to visit, but Pittsburgh was where she belonged.

MORGAN HAD A EUREKA MOMENT as she stood looking at Mark's receptionist. Well, not exactly at Mark's receptionist, but at the collection of photographs behind the woman.

"Ms. Miller. Mr. Jameson will take you right back."

Mark's face lit up when he let her into the office. "Morgan, what a pleasant surprise. I was expecting your mother." He gestured toward the couch and she took a seat.

"Mom asked me to come again. And it finally hit me, the missing piece."

"Missing piece?"

"You see, I couldn't quite figure it out why you were

so intent on buying the business. Don't get me wrong, it has a lot of potential for growth, but it's not quite in the same league as most of your purchases."

"We're always looking for new—"

Her laughter interrupted him. "Save the spiel. Like I said, I figured out why you want the store. It's not so much about the business as it is about the building."

She opened her briefcase. "I'd already found this." She handed him computer printouts. "In the last five years, Jameson, Inc. has purchased a number of businesses in Oakland, all of them on Forbes or Fifth. And if I drove by those businesses today, I'll bet I'd find new high-rises that now house students, not just from your alma mater, but from the other universities nearby."

He nodded. "You've been doing your homework."

"Well, some. But I didn't put it all together until I saw the pictures behind your receptionist's desk. Which means if my mother does decide to sell OCDR to you, the price has just gone up substantially. And we'd want a guarantee that even if you build on the property, there will still be an office for the store, that you'll honor your agreement to continue to employ Sunny and my mom."

Morgan wasn't sure what sort of reaction she'd expected, but when he chuckled, she knew that wasn't it. "Morgan, I told you I was a good judge of talent. The job offer is still on the table, but the salary has taken a substantial jump. As for this—" he waved the paper "—if your mother is interested in selling, your terms would be agreeable. I'll find new space for the store to work out of while we're building, but OCDR will be back at its current location as soon as possible."

She stood. "Thanks, Mark."

"My pleasure. Not my accountant's pleasure, but mine. I really do hope you'll reconsider my job offer. I—"

She didn't let him finish. "Thanks, but I'm heading back to San Diego."

Her mother's offer flitted through her mind, but she quickly pushed it away.

She was going to call on Monday and accept one of the jobs in San Diego. It's what she'd worked for. It's what she wanted…wasn't it?

CHAPTER TWENTY-FOUR

E.J., I'm heading out in a minute for one last wedding with Conner. I've had such a good time playing his girl Friday. And though I wouldn't want to do it as a full-time job, I realize I'm going to miss it…miss him.

THE NEXT NIGHT, AT MORGAN'S LAST reception with Conner, she asked an embarrassed looking Tessa and a not-so-embarrassed looking Nikki, "Again?" As a matter of fact, Nikki looked beyond pleased with herself.

"You can't tell me that ending up at the wedding I'm working was just another coincidence," Morgan declared.

"I wasn't planning to try to feed you that line. You're too smart for that." Nikki grinned, unashamed. "We asked your mom where you'd be. Figured we should help you see your last wedding out with a bang."

"*Bang* is just another word for *thud*. I swear, if Conner catches on…" Morgan let the threat die, because it was obviously not having the desired effect. Nikki was still grinning.

"So, have you noticed any likely male candidates for us? Men with potential?" she asked.

"*Man,* not men. As in a singular man for Nikki, because I'm not looking for a new one. Not looking for an old one, either. Basically, I'm not looking," Tessa muttered. "I'm just here to try and rein her in."

"You're not doing such a great job," Morgan assured her.

"Tell me about it. But I notice you don't seem to have any better luck than I do. After all, she's never gotten me questioned by the cops and other various law enforcement groups."

"Hey." Nikki waved her hand. "I'm still here and I can hear you both."

"We intended for you to hear," Tessa stated. "Not that we expect you to listen."

Nikki stuck out her tongue in a not so very adult way, then turned back to Morgan, obviously ignoring Tessa, who was muttering about how immature she was. "So, what about it? Any signs of available men?"

"You crash my last reception *and* you want me to play your pimp?" Morgan wasn't sure if she was flattered that Nikki trusted her opinion, or insulted that her friend would even ask.

Flattered won out.

There was just no way to be insulted or even stay annoyed with Nikki. Her zest for adventure was contagious.

Tessa didn't seem to find it quite as hard to be annoyed with Nikki. Her displeasure was obvious as she grumbled, "Pimping for your friends. Another great column idea, Nikki."

Nikki either missed Tessa's annoyance or ignored it. She simply zeroed in on what she wanted to hear. "Hey, you're right. That's a great topic. After all, what if you find a great guy, a nice guy, who doesn't do anything for you? Why should you just toss him aside when you can pass him on to a friend?"

Immediately, Mark came to Morgan's mind. The very business-minded man and…Tessa, maybe? The idea bore some consideration.

"You're impossible." Though the sentence was a borderline growl, Tessa's affection and amusement was obvious in her tone.

"So have you spotted any likely candidates?" Nikki pressed.

Morgan bowed to the inevitable. "See the guys standing near the head table? They're in the wedding party. I overheard a couple of ladies commenting that they were doctors, and I haven't seen them with dates."

"Doctors?" Nikki asked, a light in her eyes. "Two single doctors. It's fate, Tess."

"Gee, thanks, Morgan." Tessa looked unimpressed.

"Sorry," Morgan said. "But just think about what a great column this will make for Nikki. She'll probably win some kind of journalism award."

"Oh, that would be so sweet," Nikki murmured. "An award and a doctor."

"Yeah," Morgan continued, more to egg Tessa on

than anything else. "Instead of party crashing, you can call it party pimping."

"Keep on helping me," Tessa muttered. "I'm going to owe you big time, and you know I always pay my debts."

Morgan laughed, then realized she wouldn't have to worry. She was leaving soon. Tessa wouldn't have a chance to pay her back.

"Well, why are you waiting around with me?" she asked. "Go get them."

"Come on, Tess. I've got a man who needs to be examined. A prescription I've got to fill. An ache I need cured." Nikki grabbed her hand and pulled her toward the men in question.

Tessa threw a help-me look at Morgan, who simply shrugged.

"Thanks, I'll remember this," Tess promised before the two were swallowed up by the crowd.

"So, are you ever going to introduce me to your friends?" Conner practically whispered in her ear, his breath hot against her neck.

Morgan jumped and tried to convince herself the shiver climbing up her spine was because she'd been startled, and not because of desire. But even though that's what she tried to tell herself, she didn't believe it.

She'd gone to Conner's last night after her meeting with Mark. They'd barely said two words before clothing was flying helter-skelter, leaving a trail from the front entryway to Conner's room.

She'd stayed until he was asleep, and crept out early, knowing she had to get home to let Gilligan out. At least that was her excuse. Truth was, she wanted to put off discussing her trip and her upcoming move as long as possible. The dog made a good excuse.

She'd called and left Conner a message saying she'd drive herself to this one last wedding.

She knew she could stall for only so long. She was going to have to tell him about the job. Tell him she was leaving.

But later. Not now.

"Morgan?" he said, pulling her from her thoughts. "About that introduction to your friends?"

"Friends?" she asked, trying to sound puzzled.

"The two women you were talking to just now. We've seen them at other weddings."

"They must be popular to be invited to so many weddings. Not that I would know."

He gave her a skeptical glance and she knew he knew, and even if she denied it until the cows came home, he'd still know. "Fine. Yes, they're friends. And I have nothing to do with them being here. Oh, maybe I'm responsible for them chasing after those doctors, but not for them being here."

"No, the bride and groom are responsible for them being here, right?"

He knew. She could see it in his eyes. "Well, about that. I confess, they're crashing. But I had nothing to do with that. Nothing at all."

"Really? They just happen to show up at the weddings you're working with me? It's all some big coincidence?"

"Are you calling me a liar?" He was treading dangerous ground, but she wasn't sure he knew it.

"I'm not sure. Are you? You realize I could lose the job if people found out I'd brought along a horde of people to the receptions and allowed them to crash the party. I have a reputation, which is why I work some of the most prestigious weddings in the area."

"I had nothing to do with the two of them being here." But it was her fault they were crashing. She'd been the one to mention it, and give them the idea. "Well, if you're so worried about your job, I'll leave, and you'll be in the clear."

"Morgan, I didn't mean—"

"Never mind. I'll talk to you later, Conner. Thanks for the help. I think my mom's going to sell the place, but I appreciated the opportunity to study the market and give her another option." She gathered up her things. "Goodbye."

"MORGAN," CONNER CALLED HELPLESSLY as she stormed out of the reception.

He thought about going after her, but at that moment, the mother of the bride waved him down.

He'd go after Morgan later, and they'd sort this all out.

As he worked the reception, he kept thinking about Morgan. About what they had. Last night had been amazing. To be honest, his whole time with Morgan had been amazing.

He didn't want it to end like this. Maybe he'd over-reacted a bit.

No maybe about it.

He hadn't asked about her trip. He didn't want to hear the details, didn't want to know she was leaving, which was absurd, because he was leaving, too.

But saying the words somehow made it more real, and he wasn't ready for reality to set in just yet.

That's why he'd picked a fight.

He watched for her friends, and later in the evening cornered them coming out of the ladies' room.

He stepped directly in front of them. "I believe we met informally at another reception. But since you're Morgan's friends, I thought I should make it official. I'm Conner."

"Tessa and Nikki." The close-cropped brunette, Tessa, eyed him warily. "Where did Morgan run off to?"

"She had a few things to attend to. I promised to keep an eye on you two."

Nikki groaned. "Listen, it's not her fault. We talked Annabelle into helping us and—"

"I'm not mad. I just wanted to introduce myself. I've met Sunny and thought it was time I met the two of you. Have a good evening, but not so good you get caught."

Before they could respond, he walked away, but not before he heard Nikki saying, "See, Morgan didn't need to worry. He wasn't a stick-in-the-mud about it. Now, where did we put our doctors?"

He wasn't sure why he wanted to meet Morgan's friends so badly. Maybe because he felt an undeniable need to find out everything he could about her. Right now he was kicking himself for raising the issue about her party-crashing friends, and not asking about her trip.

He was chomping at the bit by the time the reception wound down. He spotted Nikki and Tessa leaving with two men as he packed up as quickly as humanly possible. He drove across town to Morgan's.

Her house was dark. He turned off his car's engine and sat staring at the house, trying to decide if he should take a chance at waking her, or just wait until tomorrow.

He still didn't know what to make of their fight.

They'd agreed that theirs was a casual relationship. They were both moving on.

So why had it bothered him?

That it had was evident by the way he'd reacted to the fact that her friends had crashed.

She was right. It wasn't her fault. She wasn't responsible. He'd known that even before she told him. Still he'd struck out.

Why?

A knock on his windshield made him jump.

Morgan's mother, Annabelle, stood there. "So, should I be concerned that you're stalking my daughter?" She smiled as she said the words, taking out any sting.

"I was just trying to decide if I should risk waking her, or wait until tomorrow to apologize."

"My thoughts are it's never a good idea to wait. Apologies are best given as quickly as possible." She paused. "So, what'd you do?"

"Made an ass of myself."

"You know, men have a tendency to do that. Don't take it too hard. You can't escape your genetic heritage. It's like eye color or height. But thankfully, women are genetically predisposed to forgive them."

"Thanks…I think."

"So, what are you going to do?" she asked.

"I guess I'll go in and…"

"Grovel?"

"Yeah. I'm still not sure what happened."

Annabelle gave a quiet poor-dense-man cluck. "I know what happened. She's leaving, you're not happy. You fought. Makes perfect sense to me."

"She got the job then?"

Annabelle nodded.

Conner knew he should be pleased that Morgan had accomplished what she'd set out to do. She was heading home to San Diego to work the kind of job she'd always dreamed of. He had his own luck with that, a job at a paper doing what he'd always wanted.

They'd shared a perfect no-strings relationship, and now both were moving on.

Why didn't he feel happier about it?

"So, what are you doing outside this late?" he asked Annabelle.

"I had a date." She gave a schoolgirl sigh. "Our fifth. Okay, it's only five if you allow for multiple dates on the same day. Doesn't matter, I think he's the one."

"After only five dates? You think it can happen that fast?"

"I think, when something's right, it's right. One day, two, five, five hundred. It won't change. When I met my husband I just knew he was it. And this time as well." Annabelle leaned closer to the open window. "Listen, I shouldn't tell you this…"

"What?" Conner asked.

"She sparkles when she talks about you. I've witnessed my daughter's other infatuations over the years. She's had an ideal man, a type that attracted her. Business. All-business. Clean cut. A pressed and polished intellect."

"That's not me."

"Right. And that's why you're perfect for her. The man she thought she wanted wasn't who she really wanted. They were all just fillers, taking up space and wasting time while she waited for you. So, the question remains, what are *you* waiting for?"

"I don't know."

Annabelle stepped back, and Conner opened the car door. He got out, shut it, then leaned over and kissed Annabelle lightly on the cheek. "Thank you."

"Hey, anytime."

"And this new guy. He's a lucky man."

She laughed. "Let's hope he thinks so."

ANNABELLE WATCHED CONNER WALK UP to Morgan's front door and knock. Gilligan went crazy inside, barking. A light in the bedroom went on.

She stepped back into the shadows. No need having Morgan ask questions. Questions Annabelle wasn't ready to answer.

The front door opened, and her daughter stood, looking at Conner with a mix of apprehension and desire.

Annabelle knew she was right. Those two were perfect for each other.

Now, if only they were smart enough to recognize that fact. Conner was a man, and in Annabelle's opinion they tended to be a bit slow on the romance uptake. But Morgan? She was her mother's daughter.

Annabelle had a lot of hope that she was going to figure out where she belonged, and soon.

CHAPTER TWENTY-FIVE

E.J., what on earth is wrong with me? I'm a decisive person. I make a decision and I stick to it. Why does it feel as if I'm suddenly becoming unglued? It all boils down to two simple questions. Where is home? And an offshoot of that, what do I want?

WHEN MORGAN LET CONNER INTO her house, he'd said, without preamble, that he wanted to talk.

But she hadn't wanted to. So, rather than talking, rather than apologizing, rather than saying the myriad things on her mind, she'd kissed him, then led him to her bedroom. And she'd left before he woke up. Left him in her bed with a note on the counter saying she'd be back.

She needed to get out for a while before she told Conner she was leaving Pittsburgh.

Maybe that is what home is, Morgan mused as she

stood outside the diner, looking through the window at her friends. *It's knowing there's somewhere that you always belonged.*

Gina, Nikki, Tess and Sunny.

They were sitting at the same table they'd sat at for so many years, talking, laughing. Knowing they were home.

Home.

Happy.

Morgan could leave tonight and not come back for years, and when she did she knew she'd be accepted unquestionably.

She walked in.

"Hey, there you are." Gina's expression was still tentative.

Morgan shot her a genuine smile in return, hoping it reassured her. "Good morning, all." She looked at Nikki, wearing her standard Sunday morning glasses. "How did the crashing go last night?"

"Great. We have a double date with the doctors next Friday, and I have a great column for this week," she replied.

"And we've agreed no more crashing," Tessa assured her. "Right, Nikki?"

Their friend looked less than enthused, but she nodded.

"So we won't risk getting you in trouble again," Tessa finished.

"It doesn't matter. That was my last wedding. I'm done. Done with just about everything but the packing. I've given Mom my outline for the store's possible futures and she's decided to sell."

"Oh." All four of her friends looked disappointed,

and Morgan wasn't sure if it was that she was done with the weddings or that Annabelle was selling the store.

"So, you are definitely leaving," Sunny said, a statement more than a question.

"Yep. Both firms in San Diego offered me a job, so I have my choice. I said I'd let them know tomorrow. Both are great firms, definitely a bump up from what I was doing at LM Co."

No one said anything.

"It's what I've worked for since college, and they're both great opportunities."

She wasn't sure if she was trying to convince them or herself. "So, Sunny, is Ian all settled into his new apartment? I've heard through the grapevine that you've been spending a lot of time over there."

It was a blatant attempt to shift the focus of the conversation, but Morgan didn't care. She'd hoped talking her job options over with her friends would help clarify things, but now she didn't think it would.

"Yes, he's all settled." This time it was obvious that Sunny wanted to change the topic. "So, Nikki, what about your—"

"Uh, uh, uh." Nikki tsked. "We want to know. Just what's going on with you and Ian?"

"Nothing. I mean, we're friends. That's all." Sunny's face turned a delicate shade of pink.

No one else said anything.

"Fine. Maybe there's a little something, but we're not dating. I mean, not exactly. Johnny's been with us, so that's not dating, right? We're friends. I mean, I thought that's all we were until last night."

"Last night?" Tessa prompted.

"He kissed me."

"Kissed you on the cheek, as in, thanks for all the help?" Nikki asked.

Sunny shook her head.

"Kissed you like he meant it?" Gina pressed.

"Like he meant it. And I guess I meant it, too, because I kissed him back."

"Then I'd say, Johnny or no Johnny, you're dating," Nikki declared. "And I'm the resident dating expert here. I should know. But let's poll the table. Tessa?"

"Yes, definitely dating."

"Gina?"

"No ifs, ands or buts."

"Morgan?"

Morgan added her agreement. They teased each other, laughed as they shared the this-and-thats from their weeks.

THE HARDEST PART ABOUT LEAVING Pittsburgh would be leaving these women. Even Gina. Morgan loved her friends in San Diego, but she couldn't imagine ever finding something like this there.

She said goodbye just as she had every Sunday that she'd come to brunch. A casual see-you-soon. But she knew—and her friends knew—*soon* could be quite a while.

"You did good." Sunny was the last one still standing outside the diner under the awning. "I'm glad you two made up."

"Me, too."

"We're going to miss you, Morgan. *I'm* going to miss you. I liked having you back at the brunches, and puttering around the shop. Having you home has been wonderful."

"But I'll be back for visits. I'll make sure my trips include a Sunday."

"But it won't be quite the same."

Morgan looked through the diner's window. The waitress was clearing off the remains of their brunch. Then she looked back at Sunny. "No, it won't be quite the same. But it's time for me to go home."

They hugged and Sunny left.

Morgan stood another few moments on the sidewalk just drinking in the sights and sounds of the city.

She had an apology to give, one more goodbye to make. Then it would be time to leave.

CONNER ROLLED OVER IN BED AND threw his arm over Morgan. Rather than sleep-warmed skin, he felt fur.

Slowly he opened his eyes and found himself looking at Gilligan. The bulldog wasn't the prettiest picture at the best of times. This moment, facing the dog's less-than-optimum side, was the worst.

Conner pulled his arm back and rolled out of bed in practically one motion.

He found his way to the kitchen and spotted Morgan's note on the counter: "Brunch with my friends. Be back in a bit. Make yourself at home."

He'd just got dressed when Morgan returned.

"Morning," she said.

"Morning."

"I hope you didn't mind that I snuck out to meet my friends."

"No. I just woke up, grabbed a shower and was going to head home."

"Oh."

"I've got a lot to do. I wanted to tell you—no, I didn't want to tell you, just like I didn't want to ask about your trip. Once we've said the words…" He shook his head, then in a rush said, "I'm leaving next week. I've got one last reception next weekend."

"I have a job waiting in San Diego. I just have to call and accept, then make my arrangements."

"So, I imagine you've got a lot to do as well."

"Tons. I don't have much to pack. Most of my stuff is in storage in San Diego. But I have to contact a real estate agent for selling this house, and I have to book a flight."

"What day are you leaving?"

"I thought I'd head to San Diego on Friday or Saturday. I'd like to take my time finding a new place before I start work. And finding someplace that will let me have pets might be tricky."

"So it's over." This was perfect. Conner should be overjoyed things were working out so well for both of them. But for some reason, he wasn't. "It's just like we said it would be."

"We've both done exactly what we set out to do. We've got our dream jobs lined up, and we've had fun together. As busy as we're both going to be, I guess this is goodbye."

"We could do dinner or something next week," he offered.

She shook her head. "I think it's probably better if we just make a clean break right now. I'm not really into lengthy goodbyes."

He wasn't into lengthy goodbyes either, but he wasn't sure if he was ready for one this abrupt. But ready or not, he slowly nodded. "You're right. I just want to say it's been fun."

Awkward. Why did he feel so awkward?

"This is ridiculous. Come here." He held his arms out, and the tightness seemed to evaporate as Morgan walked into them. They hugged for a long time. "This has been amazing."

"Yes."

"Well, goodbye, Morgan. Good luck with the new job."

"I'll be watching the papers for your photographs. If you're ever in southern California, look me up."

"Same if you're in D.C." He opened the door, but hesitated before he walked out. "Goodbye."

"Goodbye, Conner."

Conner walked to his car. He'd never had a relationship end so amicably. He should be relieved.

Instead he felt…

He didn't know exactly what he felt, but it wasn't relief.

It wasn't even excitement about the new job.

His dream job, the one he'd put on hold for the last couple of years. He should be thrilled he'd heard back so quickly, that Luke was right, the job was his.

Should be…but wasn't quite. And he didn't have a clue why that was or what to do about it.

CHAPTER TWENTY-SIX

E.J., I called Ellie Marx and accepted the job at Turner, Inc. I'm spending the week making my arrangements here. I've got a flight out Saturday morning. Thanks for offering a room while I apartment shop. It's good to be coming back where I belong...Morgan

Morgan, you're sure you know what you're doing? E.J.

THE WEEK WAS CRAZY BUSY. But by Friday, Morgan looked at the two suitcases and the four boxes she was taking to her mom's to be shipped when she'd found a new apartment.

The auctioneer was prowling the house, making notes on a tablet.

Everything was done. She'd said her goodbyes, had a flight in the morning that would take her back to San Diego and her challenging new job. The type of job that had been her goal when she graduated from college.

She'd made it.

Life was back on track. She'd checked off items on her list and everything was in order. Her life was perfect.

Perfectly awful.

Her mother was on her way to Mark's office to sign away the OCDR. Tess had okayed the contract. Conner was packing to move to D.C. and start his new job.

Yes, perfectly awful.

In a moment of sudden clarity and honesty, Morgan finally admitted what she'd suspected for quite a while now.

She didn't want to leave.

"Lady, you're right, there are some nice pieces here, which means I'm able to offer you significantly more than I normally would." He stated a figure that even Morgan knew was absurdly low.

"Thank you, but I've changed my mind." She hadn't known she was going to say the words until they tumbled out of her mouth. She almost expected the earth to move, or at the very least the heavens to open and shoot a bolt of lightning at her. After all, who in their right mind decided not to accept the job of their dreams? The job they'd spent their entire adult life working toward?

But nothing happened as Morgan said the most monumentally important words she'd ever uttered. The earth didn't shake off its axis…nothing. Nothing except Morgan suddenly felt lighter than she had in a long time.

The auctioneer gave her a significantly higher quote.

"I'm sorry. I've decided I'm not leaving Pittsburgh. I'm not moving. This is home."

Uncle Auggie's house with its eclectic supply of clutter, antiques and geriatric pets was home. Pittsburgh was home. Living next door to her mother, going to Sunday brunches…it was all part of being home.

Morgan wanted a chance to see if her mom's new friend grew into something more, if her party crashing ways were finally over. She wanted to see what happened between Sunny and Ian, and wanted to be there when Tessa and Nikki each found someone. She wanted to rebuild a friendship with Gina and Thomas.

Conner?

She wanted Conner, but she couldn't keep him from his dreams. But she could be honest with him and let him know that what they'd had was more than just casual to her.

And…

She realized that the auctioneer was still talking to her, quoting ever higher prices, at the same time that she realized her mother could be signing the papers at Mark's right now.

"I'm sorry," Morgan said as she started to usher the man toward the door, snagging her purse and keys on the way.

"But no matter what you quote, I'm not selling."

She got him out on the porch, locked the door and sprinted to her car, even as she rooted in her bag for her cell phone.

She grabbed it, hit speed-dial one and listened as she got in the car, started it and backed out of the drive.

The auctioneer was still standing on the porch, looking unsure what to do.

"Really, I'm not selling, but thank you," she called out.

Her mother picked up the phone.

"Mom, it's Morgan. Have you signed the papers…?"

CONNER TRIED TO TURN HIS SCOWL into a smile. He was working, after all. His last wedding. He walked around the reception, taking this shot or that. Glasses clanged; the bride and groom kissed.

He snapped the shot and tried not to remember his last kiss with Morgan. It hadn't been anything near that passionate. A brief kiss, a thanks for everything, then it was over.

He was furious, more at himself than at her. After all, he'd set the casual-only rule, and she'd followed it to the letter.

He should be thankful that they'd had so much fun and that it had ended well. She'd told him if he was ever in southern California to look her up.

Look her up.

Something you might say to a casual friend, someone you don't expect to keep in contact with. Someone who might be associated with a fond memory or two but who had no real emotional tie.

Look me up.

The father of the bride was dancing with his daughter. Conner took the obligatory shots.

But he knew his heart wasn't in it. All he could think about was Morgan. He wished…

He wished they'd had more time.

His film began to rewind and he headed back to his supply case with a sense of relief. This was almost done.

This chapter of his life. He'd start his new job and things would get back to normal.

As he approached the back of the hall, he spotted her.

"Morgan." He realized he'd spoken out loud, but she didn't stir.

He came up behind her. "So what's a woman like you doing lurking in a dark corner?"

She turned slowly, her eyes locking with his. "Just enjoying the sights."

"Morgan…" he began, but she held up a finger to his lips, silencing him.

"I know I'm crashing, but I needed to tell you something. I won't keep you long. Don't say anything. Just listen, please."

"But—"

"Please?"

He nodded.

Morgan pulled him into the corner. It had been so easy on her way over. She'd planned out what she had to say, but now that she was here, standing next to him, the words she'd so painstakingly worked on evaporated.

She ran her hand over his slightly stubbled cheek, looking for the right way to say what needed to be said. "I have a few confessions to make. I've lied to you from the beginning. Hell, that's not a surprise, I've lied to myself for a long time as well. I need to tell you, to apologize."

He looked as if he was about to say something, but she held her index finger up again.

"That first wedding? I wasn't a guest. I crashed it. Oh, I didn't mean to crash…Annabelle tricked me into it, but still. And when I saw you, there was this spark. I didn't know how to just say, 'hey, you, you do some-

thing to me, for me. Let's see if you can do some more.'
So I made up a reason to see you again."

"Your mother wasn't looking at expanding the
store?" he asked.

"No. Not then. It was just an excuse. She really
wanted to sell. She didn't like being in charge."

He was frowning.

"And my friends who crashed the weddings we
worked? I didn't tell them where we'd be, that was
my—"

"Your mother again?"

Morgan nodded. "But I put the idea of crashing in
their heads. All that isn't the worst of it. When I told
you that I was leaving town, that I wanted to keep us
casual…when I said the words, I didn't know they were
all a lie, but they were. Big lies. I'm not leaving. I'm
staying here in Pittsburgh. I'm going to stay in the
house Uncle Auggie left me, a house that's become
home. I'm going to keep Gilligan, the aging humping
dog, and the two mysteriously vanishing cats. I stopped
Mom from signing the papers and selling the business
to Mark. We're going to work out terms and I'm going
to buy OCDR. What started out as a lie, one I used to
have an excuse to see you, has grown into more."

The words had come out in a breathless rush. She
took a deep breath and dived back in before she lost her
nerve. "I can see it all, Conner. I can see all the things
the store can become. I'm going to subcontract with
other local businesses. Customers will be able to order
invitations, flowers, even a photographer through
OCDR. The world is so busy, and having one place to
go to get everything, well, it's a great marketing hook."

"I'm happy for you, Morgan." He paused. "Is that it?"

"No. There's one more lie I have to clear up. I'll confess, it's the biggest one I told. I thought little white lies couldn't hurt anyone. When I initially said I wanted to keep us casual, I meant it. But gradually, it became apparent that you were more than that. Much more. You see, I'm pretty sure I love you. I'm not sure how or why. I have a type. All-business, pressed and polished. You consider shaving once a week at best. Your sense of style consists of…well, I'm pretty sure you went out and bought a lifetime supply of black T-shirts and denim. You're not my type. But I love you. It's a new and fragile love that I'm sure I'll recover from. I know you're leaving, and nothing in me wants to hold you back. It's just I couldn't go on lying to myself, or to you. I thought I wanted to make it big in business. To go back to California and climb the corporate ladder. But my mother was right—sometimes what we think we want isn't what we want at all. I'm staying in Pittsburgh and running the family store. And I understand you're leaving, but I didn't want all these lies tainting our memories. I love you, and I hope you find what you're looking for."

"Do I get to talk now?"

Morgan knew if she didn't make her escape she was going to ruin her very nice little speech by breaking down and crying. If she lost control, she might say the words she was holding back.

Stay with me.

She couldn't do that to him, couldn't ask, because she did love him. The feeling had come on fast. Probably too fast. But it was there. Big and bold.

And because she loved him, she had to let him have his dream.

He'd given it up once because Ian had needed him. She wouldn't be the reason he gave it up a second time.

"No. You don't need to say anything. I've got to go." She leaned forward and kissed his stubbly cheek. "Thank you."

"For what?"

"For being you. For giving me such beautiful memories."

She hurried out of the reception hall just as the guests started tapping their glasses again, asking the happy couple for another kiss. It felt like a scene from one of those old black-and-white movies, and she didn't want to look back.

She felt as if she'd set things to rights. She would miss Conner, but at least now that she'd told him the truth, she could look back at their time together and not have the weight of her fibs hanging over her.

And his leaving was probably for the best.

She was going to be very busy with OCDR. There was so much to do.

She was just going to ignore the fact her heart was breaking, and concentrate on the task at hand. She was going to turn Oakland Chair and Dish Rental into the premier party supply store in Pittsburgh.

She would set up meetings next week with local printers, and local photographers who might be interested in subcontracting with Oakland...

Oakland Party Supply and Rental?

OPSR?

An unexpected flash of pain struck, but Morgan pushed it back.

She loved Conner, and she'd said goodbye and let him chase after what he wanted.

She understood what that meant and truly hoped he'd find it.

CHAPTER TWENTY-SEVEN

E.J., I did it. The attorney rushed the papers through, and today I'm owner of Oakland Chair and Dish Rental, soon to be named the Party Store or Oakland Party Center or... Well, I'm still working on the name. I think that about sums up what I hope to accomplish here. One-stop party shopping. Rentals, invitations, disc jockeys, band demos, flowers...even a photographer. Speaking of which, I haven't heard from Conner. Not that I expected to, but still...

THREE WEEKS LATER, MORGAN WAS back at the diner. It was part of her new rhythm. Well, more like an old rhythm she'd quite happily fallen back into.

Nikki was regaling them with her newest exploits. She'd given up party crashing after telling them her doctor date didn't pan out. "I hope he makes it as a surgeon, 'cause he was all-hands."

Nikki had decided to try her own hand at ten-minute dating last night. "...ten minutes and you'd barely gotten past the what-do-you-do-for-a-living-and-for-fun minutia, and that stupid bell would ding."

"At least you got a column out of it," Sunny chirped.

"Shh," Nikki said. "Remember, Sunday mornings are time when anyone speaking over a whisper should be shot."

"If you didn't drink, it wouldn't be such a problem," Sunny said in a chiding motherly tone.

"Just because you have a kid doesn't mean you get to lecture me," Nikki groused.

"Nikki doesn't," Tessa said.

"Tessa," Nikki hissed.

"Doesn't what?" Morgan asked, eyeing her friend's sunglasses suspiciously. For the life of her, she couldn't think of many things that fell under the heading Nikki Doesn't Do.

Even though they couldn't see her eyes, no one at the table could miss that Nikki was glaring at Tessa, who seemed totally unperturbed as she laughed. "Nikki gave up drinking a long while back. I just realized it these last few weeks as she dragged me around crashing receptions. She doesn't drink when she's out. The hangover-on-Sunday bit was just tradition. I don't think she wanted to disappoint us, so she kept shushing and grousing, and routinely wears her dark glasses not to shield her sensitive eyes, but to cover the fact they're not the least bit bloodshot."

"Take off your glasses," Gina ordered.

"Yeah!" Sunny agreed.

"You're not hungover?" Morgan asked.

Nikki pushed the glasses up onto her head and exposed her very bright, clear eyes. "I gave up excess drinking a couple years ago. I hated losing my Sundays to a hangover."

"She needs the time because she's working on a book," Tessa shared.

"A book?" everyone else at the table repeated together, Nikki now the total focus of the morning.

Nikki shot a few daggers at Tessa with her eyes, then slowly nodded. "I've taken some of my favorite columns and expanded on them. I was going to call it *A Single Girl's Dating Guide,* but thanks to Morgan and her mom, I've changed the working title to *Confessions of a Party Crasher.*"

All her friends started laughing, and Sunny went so far as to clap. They all talked at once, assuring Nikki of her brilliance, and her successful future as a writer. The noise level rose, and everyone showered her with praise and support…except from Tessa's corner of the table. She'd gotten very quiet as she stared beyond Morgan at something, a slow smile playing on her face.

Morgan turned. Her mother had walked into the diner with an older guy and Conner in tow.

"Hi, girls." Annabelle looked positively gleeful. Her mom being that happy made Morgan nervous.

Very nervous.

Her mom being here with Conner? Even more nervous than that.

Morgan frowned as her mother pulled a chair up to the table. Her gentleman friend followed suit. Then

Morgan gazed at Conner, but he made no sign so she was at a loss as to what that was about.

"I know we're crashing your brunch, but I wasn't going to miss this for anything," Annabelle stage-whispered to the women.

CONNER DIDN'T SAY ANYTHING.

He couldn't.

He'd had a host of things he wanted to say to Morgan, had spent the night going over and over them, but all his preparation was amounting to nothing, because now that he was here in front of her, all those carefully planned words evaporated.

"Conner?" When he didn't respond, she repeated, "Conner, what did you want?"

Okay, what was first? Her name. Morgan. Even in his slightly dazed state he was sure he could get that out. "Morgan, I—"

"I heard him pull in at your place and hurried out. When I told him you weren't at home, he looked so disappointed. Then he said he had something to tell you. Well, of course, being the empathetic person I am, I offered to help him find you, and came along for the show. I brought Todd along. Say hi to Morgan's friends, Todd."

"Hi," the older gentleman said, a soft hint of the South in his voice. "Pleased to meet y'all. Especially you, Morgan. Your mama does nothing but sing your praises."

"I can't help it that my daughter is exceptional," Annabelle said. "And her friends, too, of course."

"Of course," Todd agreed.

Conner noticed that Morgan didn't seem to be

paying any attention to her mother and Todd. Her eyes hadn't left him.

"Conner?" she repeated. "Aren't you supposed to be in D.C.?"

"I could counter by asking aren't you supposed to be in San Diego?" He nodded at the table. "If you'd all excuse us, I need to borrow Morgan for a minute."

"Oh, no you don't," Annabelle said. "I crashed this brunch in order to be a witness, and I know Morgan's friends would want to be as well."

"Mom," Morgan said.

"It's fine," Conner told her. "I got to D.C. and started at the paper. I realized it wasn't what I thought it would be. I remembered what you said, that sometimes what we think we want isn't what we want at all—"

"Actually, I said it first," Annabelle announced. "Just to keep the record straight."

"You've got a smart mother, Morgan. It's true, the last couple of years I've regretted turning down my big break at photojournalism. I wanted to see the world and tell its story. But when you saw my pictures in the darkroom, you pointed out that I'd been doing that all along, after a fashion. All those weddings. I captured this particular couple's story, shared in that very special event. You showed me though it's not breaking news, it's an important story to tell. Love matters. It counts. And the nature shots are just another way of telling the story—what we've done, are doing to the environment, and to the animals that share it with us. I've spent so much time lamenting the fact I wasn't involved in the big stories. But it struck me all at once that I had been doing just that— telling stories that mattered. And I'd been happy doing it. When this job came along, I took it because it's what I thought I wanted, what I did want once upon a time. But now…"

Conner paused and Morgan sucked in her breath. She looked around the table. Her friends leaned forward, as if not to miss a single word. Her mother sat next to the gray-haired, bushy-browed gentleman with the very kind eyes.

And Conner. Conner stood there looking so good. "And now?" she prompted when the pregnant pause had gone on far too long.

"Now," he said, taking her hand. "I realize that I want to be here, want to keep taking my nature photos, and even do the occasional wedding. That's why I'm back."

"For photography?" she asked, feeling more than slightly disappointed.

He nodded. "You see, I hear Oakland Chair and Dish Rental is in the process of expanding its party offerings, and I thought you might like to hire an experienced wedding photographer to help set up that portion of it."

"You want a job?" Her head felt thick, as if she were listening to him through pudding.

"That's secondary. What I really want is a chance with you. I think what we have, what we could have, deserves some time, don't you?"

Annabelle kicked her. "Say yes, honey."

Time. More time with Conner, exploring what they had? "Yes," Morgan said. "Yes."

Conner looked around the table, then back at her. "Remember what you told me at the last party you crashed?"

She nodded.

"Me, too."

"What did you say?" Sunny asked, to a chorus of *yeah, tell us.*

"Pittsburgh is home," Morgan replied.

"She did say that," Conner agreed. "But what I was referring to was when you said you loved me. Me, too."

"You love yourself?" Sunny frowned.

"I love Morgan," Morgan clarified, smiling.

"So, am I invited to brunch?" Conner asked.

Everyone said yes at once, Morgan's was loudest and another chair was located. The five friends, plus Morgan's mother and Todd, squished together to accommodate Conner.

He took Morgan's hand under the table as they all talked and talked—sharing, laughing.

This, Morgan thought. This was exactly what she wanted. Her family, her friends…and Conner. Always Conner.

Sometimes what you think you want isn't what you want after all, she reminded herself.

But sometimes…sometimes it was.

E.J., so there it is. I'm here in Pittsburgh, busy at the store, with my friends and Conner. Things are going well between us. Actually, each day with him is a gift. But I miss you. Any chance you'd like to come visit Pittsburgh? I know this great little diner on Fifth Avenue. We could do breakfast. And I could introduce you to my friends. Especially Nikki. I really think there's a chance you two could hit it off. She has a thing for doctors. I finally fixed up Tessa and Mark, and they're going strong. Maybe matchmaking is my true calling. Come visit and we'll see if I'm right.

And if I am? Well, we do have hospitals in Pittsburgh you could work at.

In the meantime, I'm happy. Oh, I'm not exactly doing what I thought I'd be doing, but you know, this is one case of my mother being right. Sometimes what you think you want, isn't what you want at all. But I finally figured out what I want and where I belong. I don't think life gets any better than that.

Everything you love about romance…
and more!

Please turn the page for Signature Select™
Bonus Features.

Confessions
of a
Party
Crasher

**BONUS
FEATURES
INSIDE**

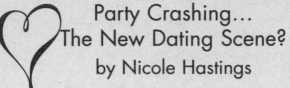

Party Crashing...
The New Dating Scene?
by Nicole Hastings

(from Confessions of a Party Crasher)

Part Three of Six

Party-Crashing Etiquette 101

In part one and two of this series we've established why I started crashing parties, and gave you a list of types of parties that might easily be crashed and can involve eligible men. Now let's talk party-crashing etiquette.

Etiquette? you ask. Well, yes. Even if you're going to a party uninvited there's no reason to be rude about it. I've found three basic rules really make the entire party-crashing experience better for both the crasher and the crashees.

BIGGER IS BETTER: Look for parties that are big enough to absorb an extra guest without anyone noticing: wedding receptions, graduation parties, anniversary celebrations, even big family reunions (you can always be Uncle Jonas's secret love child). And all those big milestone parties: Bar Mitzvahs, Bat Mitvzahs, quinceañeras, sweet-sixteen parties... Anywhere where you can join in without standing out.

I went to a quinceañera a few weeks ago. Talk about fun. As dressy and formal as a wedding, but when the girl leaves, she doesn't have a husband in tow...just fond memories of a big party that was all about her. I had fond memories of the party, as well, namely Alejandro. Al was a perfect gentleman...while his mama was in the room. But later, when he walked me to my car? I knew I'd be crashing something again the next weekend.

MAKING AN ENTRANCE: Never, I mean, never, crash until after the food has been served. The meal has been planned for a certain number and you weren't one of that number. So, stop and eat at McDonald's, and crash the party late. The fact that you're crashing shouldn't cost the hosts anything but some dance-floor space. If they have an open bar, don't drink. But if you can pay for your own, have at it.

LEARN THE CUSTOMS: Once you have a target, do your homework. For a recently crashed Jewish wedding, I learned the Hava Nagila dance and how to say mazel tov. A Polish wedding? Definitely know the polka. And really, just about any wedding, regardless of the ethnicity, requires the ability to do the Electric Slide!

You see, even when breaking the rules, there are rules that should be followed.

Tomorrow's Column: Party Pimping
So you go fishing in the dating pool and find a nice man who doesn't really do it for you. Why throw him back? Pass him on to a friend...

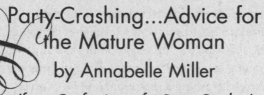

Party-Crashing…Advice for the Mature Woman
by Annabelle Miller
(from Confessions of a Party Crasher)

(As told during a speech to a Red Hat Society Group)

Thank you, for *inviting* me to be with you tonight. We're all women, something our daughters like to forget. At least, mine would. When she was little she thought I hung the moon. I'd say, *I love you so much I could burst with it.* I knew our relationship was changing the day I said it and she looked at me and replied, *Just don't go bursting in front of my friends.* That was the day my moon set. I was no longer amazing, I was embarrassing.

And embarrassed was how she felt when I took her out on the town. Granted, it wasn't quite a town…it was a wedding reception we crashed. But I was hoping she'd meet some man back here in Pittsburgh and stick around. I didn't want her to go back to San Diego. I missed her. What mother wouldn't miss her daughter and want her to move back home?

Finding her a new boyfriend here in town seemed like the logical solution. But how to introduce her to someone? Taking her clubbing... well, that wouldn't be very mommish. But a nice wedding reception? You see, years ago I met my husband crashing a reception. And I'll confess, getting my daughter a date by crashing that reception wasn't my only goal...I thought lightning might strike twice for me. After years happily on my own, I was ready for another relationship.

Well, long story short, my daughter did meet a man. Unfortunately, I didn't. It seems mature men don't go to wedding receptions unless they're with a woman who insists. There seems to be a plethora of men for the twentysomething crowd—even my daughter's friend managed to meet a man at crashed receptions. But the over fifty group? Not so much.

So, where can women of an age meet men?

I gave it a lot of thought.

One of my early tries was a wake. A good Irish wake. And there were eligible men my age there. But there's a downside to meeting men at wakes—they tend to be rather depressed. Not only that, you can depend on the fact that you are most definitely the rebound woman.

Cross off wakes.

Funerals, weddings. What other milestones are celebrated with parties big enough you can crash without being noticed?

Proms are out.

Graduation parties?

No.

Okay, nix parties. I tried a science-fiction convention. I did get drafted to serve on a ship by a very interesting captain...but unfortunately he found his role-playing more fun than playing with me.

So I borrowed my daughter's dog, Gilligan. Pet obedience classes. Maybe there'd be a nice older gentleman there. And there was. His name was Hershal and he brought along his prized toy poodle. We were getting along fine, until I realized I'd forgotten something. Back in his younger days, Gilligan had been a humper. I mean that dog humped anything and everything. But as he aged, arthritis set in and things quieted down on that front. But it seemed for Ms. Muffy, he'd made an attempt. Ms. Muffy was not impressed by poor Gilligan's attempts to resurrect his glory days, and my new friend wasn't either. I protested that the mutt wasn't even mine, which added insult to injury when Gilligan and I were kicked out of the obedience class for crashing.

So I thought about other types of classes. Maybe some kind of self-help?

I got a directory from my hospital. Parents Without Partners jumped out at me. Perfect. I was a parent. I didn't have a partner. Now, granted, my daughter is twentysomething, but still, it counts and I went. The meeting was mainly women, and the few men who joined were not only way too young, they were coping with raising kids and didn't seem to have time for a relationship.

Ladies, it was tough. Let me tell you.

The bar scene didn't work for me when I was a bar-scene age, so I had my doubts about it working now. I thought about a car-care class, but I figured the powers that be supplied me with a mechanic—someone to fix my cars. I had no interest in learning to fix them myself and didn't think I wanted a man my age who was just learning car care.

Grocery stores?

10   Bah. Same principle. I don't want a man who cooks, I want one who will take me out.

Then one day I happened upon an AA meeting. How I ended up there is a long story that involves a borrowed lab coat and an accusation of impersonating a doctor. We don't have time for it. But there I was with a room of people who used to drink and don't now, hanging out and talking about the fact they used to drink. A fun group if ever there was one.

And that's where I met my man. He has his ten-year pin. Ten years, no alcohol. I'd say that was a good bet. So, don't just sit back and hang out with each other. Self-help groups are wonderful. Oh, it might seem like people in a support group might not be the most upbeat, but some are.

And even though I'm off the market, I've been gathering suggestions from friends.

How about a gourmet club, a cigar bar? Maybe a gentleman's club...of course, you'd have to petition to be the first female member, but that would definitely garner you a bit of notice.

Maybe you could crash a biker club? I've noticed that a lot of older men, when they reach their midlife crisis, buy a bike. Might be the place to find a few. Church suppers, lawn-bowling banquet, the policeman's ball. I mean, who doesn't love uniforms? Speaking of uniforms, I've noticed a lot of reenactors' groups have sprouted up in western Pennsylvania...what about crashing one of their shindigs? Men in uniforms and you'd get to wear a pretty hooped skirt.

There are those free screening days at hospitals and pharmacies...those are bound to bring in men of a certain age. The sky's the limit.

Now, I know you allotted me more time to talk, and while I'm so glad you invited me to your meeting, I think you've got the gist of what I have to say. I know you have refreshments all laid out for when I finish, but there's an AA meeting down the hall...I bet they wouldn't notice a dozen ladies sneakin' in and sit at the back. Especially if those ladies bring along their own refreshments to share....

Falling for the Younger Man
by Christine Cowern

What woman doesn't want a hot younger man telling her she's beautiful? If you've found yourself falling for a younger man, you're not alone! More and more women (and the younger men who love them) are learning to transcend social stigmas and embrace love where they find it.

Joan Collins did it. And so did Susan Sarandon and Raquel Welch. They met, and in some cases married men more than ten years their junior. It's a tempting thought. After all, what woman doesn't want a hot young stud telling her she's beautiful? And these days more and more women (and younger men!) are jumping on the bandwagon.

So, what should you do if you've fallen (or are about to fall) for a younger man? If you put yourself first and focus on the positive, anything is possible!

The Pros

Having a relationship with a younger man can be just as fulfilling, if not more fulfilling, as dating someone older, according to Felicia Brings, coauthor of *Older Women, Younger Men: New Options for Love and Romance.* "Dating a younger man makes you feel younger. It's exciting because there's discovery," says Brings, who interviewed over two hundred couples for her book.

She says one of the reasons these relationships work is the changing perception of male/female roles. "Older women who have come up through the women's movement have rejected relationships where their husbands expect them to have dinner on the table when they come home from work," she explains.

For Susan, a successful forty-seven-year-old businesswoman, dating younger men definitely has its perks. "They aren't jaded by life's experiences. An older man is more set in his ways, whereas a younger man is more accepting of successful women." Susan should know. She's been dating younger men for fifteen years and is currently seeing someone fifteen years her junior.

Give Yourself Permission

But even if you're interested in a younger man, giving yourself permission to take it to the next level is another story, especially since stigmas still exist against these untraditional unions. "There's a tremendous double standard," says Brings.

"You can't avoid it. When you have Michael Douglas getting married to Catherine Zeta-Jones nobody questions it. The minute you have an older woman getting married to a significantly younger man, she's robbing the cradle."

In fact, eighty percent of the women Brings interviewed had no idea the young men in their lives were interested in them romantically. "Very often if a younger man pays attention to an older woman, she kind of dismisses him. She can't quite believe it's that kind of interest."

Instead of dismissing the relationship, Brings suggests thinking about why you are reacting the way you are. "The way a woman can empower herself is to realize she's got a right to be happy. The fact that he's a younger man doesn't mean he's necessarily right for her. But don't dismiss it just because he's younger. Recognize *those* taboos are created by men in a man's world."

Friends and Family

Once you're comfortable with your relationship, meeting each other's friends and family is the next step. It's a situation that can initially be more stressful than it is satisfying. But Brings says there are ways to turn the experience into a positive one. She suggests choosing events that accentuate what you have in common.

If he loves rock climbing, join him and his friends the next time they go. It'll give you a chance to bond while doing something you love. You can also try new activities together. Taking a pottery class for the first time will introduce you to a whole new set of mutual friends that you can both relate to. Being happy with your relationship also sends a positive message to the people around you. "If you have a couple that's happy together no matter what the age difference that happiness projects itself. In time people see it and then they become comfortable," says Brings.

Lust vs. Love

Of course, just because your younger man looks like Brad Pitt and you've got a great sexual chemistry doesn't mean it's a match made in heaven. Emotional maturity also counts for a lot, especially if there's a large age gap between you.

"I think when a guy is a lot younger, women will tend to make excuses for him," says Brings. "They'll say, 'He didn't know any better' or 'He's never experienced this.' You can't do that. You just really have to observe their behavior. If you have issues, bring them up."

For Zoe, a thirty-four-year-old writer who'd dated two younger men, emotional maturity is the key. "I met one of the younger men when we were both working abroad. He was more mature than most guys his age because he had been living abroad and was well traveled," she says. "The other man was twenty-three years old and was clearly too young for me from an emotional stand-point. He wasn't comfortable in his own skin."

Susan agrees that maturity is crucial. "When I was forty-two I met a young man who was twenty-one and we went out for four and a half years," she says. "He was very unique in that he was quite mature and worldly. I found we came together on a very strong spiritual level because he was an old soul."

Making It Last

The best piece of advice Brings has for older women who have fallen or desire to fall for younger men—just be yourself. So there's a twelve year age gap between you. Instead of comparing yourself to every twenty-year-old girl that walks by, realize that your man is attracted to you for a reason. So instead of running away, embrace what you've got.

16

It's an issue that Brings who has herself dated much younger men takes to heart. "My last boyfriend was seventeen years younger than me. Where I'm at right now, seventeen years is no big deal," she says. "When I first got involved with a younger man I was embarrassed. I felt ashamed and kept our relationship in the closet for a long time. Now I judge people as people and on their merit as human beings."

If you're with the right person you'll know it. If he happens to be young *and* gorgeous, that's just icing on the cake.

*Originally published online at www.eHarlequin.com

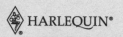

**Hidden in the secrets of antiquity,
lies the unimagined truth...**

Introducing

ROGUE ANGEL™

a brand-new line filled with mystery
and suspense, action and adventure,
and a fascinating look into history.

And it all begins with DESTINY.

In a sealed crypt in
France, where the
terrifying legend of
the beast of Gevaudan
begins to unravel,
Annja Creed discovers
a stunning artifact
that will seal her destiny.

*Available every other
month starting
July 2006, wherever
you buy books.*

GOLD
EAGLE®

GRA1

If you enjoyed what you just read,
then we've got an offer you can't resist!

Take 2 bestselling love stories FREE!

Plus get a FREE surprise gift!

Page-turning drama...

Exotic, glamorous locations...

Intense emotion and passionate seduction...

Sheikhs, princes and billionaire tycoons...

This summer, may we suggest:

THE SHEIKH'S DISOBEDIENT BRIDE
by Jane Porter

On sale June.

AT THE GREEK TYCOON'S BIDDING
by Cathy Williams

On sale July.

THE ITALIAN MILLIONAIRE'S VIRGIN WIFE

On sale August.

With new titles to choose from every month,
discover a world of romance in our books written
by internationally bestselling authors.

HARLEQUIN® *Presents*

It's the ultimate in quality romance!

Available wherever Harlequin books are sold.

www.eHarlequin.com